ANOTHER GARRISON OFF THE MARKET?

Ladies, brace yourselves! Our sources report that consummate bachelor Adam Garrison, the youngest male Garrison, is all but engaged. He was spotted at an upscale bistro with what our witness called "a rather plain blonde who appears to have stolen his heart." She wasn't sporting a ring, but our insider says it's only a matter of time. The source overheard an exchange between Adam and an elder socialite where he almost confirmed as much.

In other news, seems the sixtieth birthday party of town drunk Bonita Garrison is still set to take place at her son's nightclub, Estate, later this month. No word on why she hasn't gone into rehab yet, but let's hope she doesn't do anything at her celebration that will further tarnish the Garrison name.

Dear Reader,

This book was extraspecial for me because it gave hubby and me the perfect excuse to take our first real adults-only vacation in years. Research! We left our four sons and the dog behind—the boys didn't miss us but the dog did ☺—and traveled to South Beach. We even took a short cruise—our first—to the Bahamas.

South Beach was nothing like the laid-back North Carolina beaches I usually visit, but I did my best to give you a slice of the atmosphere. So when you get to the part about South Beach coffee shops selling condoms, they do!

I hope you can kick back, imagine the sand beneath your toes and palm fronds stirring above your head in a brisk ocean breeze and enjoy Lauryn and Adam's story.

Best,

Emilie

EMILIE ROSE

SECRETS OF THE TYCOON'S BRIDE

Published by Silhouette Books
America's Publisher of Contemporary Romance

To my husband for never saying no. Heaven knows
I've given you plenty of reasons and opportunities to do so.
You spoil me rotten. Don't think I haven't noticed.

Special thanks and acknowledgment to Emilie Rose for her
contribution to THE GARRISONS miniseries.

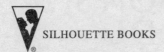 SILHOUETTE BOOKS

ISBN-13: 978-0-373-76831-8
ISBN-10: 0-373-76831-1

SECRETS OF THE TYCOON'S BRIDE

Copyright © 2007 by Harlequin Books S.A.

EMILIE ROSE

lives in North Carolina with her college sweetheart husband and four sons. Writing is Emilie's third (and hopefully her last) career. She's managed a medical office and run a home day care, neither of which offers half as much satisfaction as plotting happy endings. Her hobbies include quilting, gardening and cooking (especially cheesecake). Her favorite TV shows include *ER, CSI* and Discovery Channel's medical programs. Emilie's a country music fan, because she can find an entire book in almost any song.

Letters can be mailed to:
Emilie Rose
P.O. Box 20145
Raleigh, NC 27619
E-mail: EmilieRoseC@aol.com

THE GARRISONS

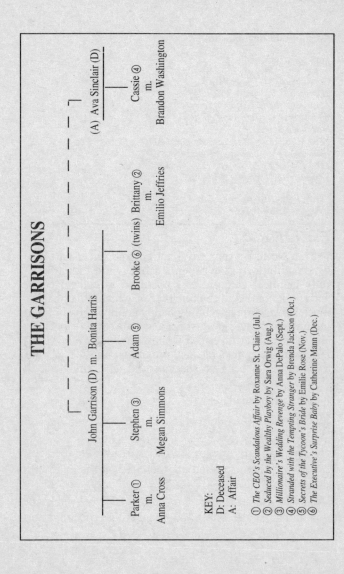

John Garrison (D) m. Bonita Harris

(A) Ava Sinclair (D)

Parker ①
m.
Anna Cross

Stephen ③
m.
Megan Simmons

Adam ⑤

Brooke ⑥ (twins)

Brittany ②
m.
Emilio Jeffries

Cassie ④
m.
Brandon Washington

KEY:
D: Deceased
A: Affair

① *The CEO's Scandalous Affair* by Roxanne St. Claire (Jul.)
② *Seduced by the Wealthy Playboy* by Sara Orwig (Aug.)
③ *Millionaire's Wedding Revenge* by Anna DePalo (Sept.)
④ *Stranded with the Tempting Stranger* by Brenda Jackson (Oct.)
⑤ *Secrets of the Tycoon's Bride* by Emilie Rose (Nov.)
⑥ *The Executive's Surprise Baby* by Catherine Mann (Dec.)

One

Lauryn Lowes would make him a perfect wife because he didn't love her and wasn't attracted to her.

Hell, Adam Garrison realized, he barely knew her.

Their bi-weekly meetings since she'd started working for him seven months ago had never allowed time for get-to-know-you chatter. She worked days when the club was closed, and he worked nights when Estate was open. He knew little about her except what he'd read on her job application.

A tap on his open door revealed the woman in question. "You wanted to see me?"

"Come in, Lauryn. Close the door. Have a seat."

She did as he instructed and perched on the edge of the visitor chair in front of his desk.

According to his lawyer, who happened to be Adam's best friend and someone whose judgment Adam trusted, Lauryn was the perfect wife candidate.

Adam's leather chair creaked as he leaned back to make his own assessment. Lauryn wasn't bad-looking. Bland. No make-up. Pale-blond hair which she always kept pinned up. An intelligent and independent worker. Otherwise he never would have hired her to handle his nightclub's multimillion-dollar books.

"Is something wrong? This isn't our usual meeting day." Lauryn pushed the narrow rectangles of her tortoiseshell glasses up her straight nose, and then with slender, ringless fingers adjusted the longish skirt of her boring navy suit.

He'd never noticed her hands before. But then he'd never considered those hands touching him. Intimately. Her short, unpainted nails were a far cry from the lacquered claws the majority of women in his life preferred.

Besides a manicure, she'd need new clothing to carry off this charade. Maybe contacts. Better shoot for a complete makeover. Otherwise no one would believe he'd chosen her out of all the fashion models and celebrities who frequented Estate and/or his bed.

He had his pick of women. Just not the type he needed for this assignment. The council already considered him a playboy. His female equivalent would not help his cause. Lauryn was far from a party girl. If she'd dated at all in the past months no one on the staff knew it. He'd asked. Discreetly, of course.

She shifted in her chair, reminding him he hadn't answered her question. That was something else he'd always admired about her. She knew how to be quiet instead of chattering endlessly.

"Nothing's wrong, Lauryn. In fact, I'd like to offer you a raise and a…promotion of sorts." He punctuated that with what he hoped would be a reassuring smile. Whether for her or for himself, he couldn't say.

God knows he had reservations about this plan. He was

only thirty and he *liked* being single. Between witnessing his parents' far-from-perfect union and his front-row seat to the nightly dating safaris at the club, he'd never planned to marry for any reason, but he couldn't see any other way to achieve his goals.

He wanted a bigger stake in the family business and there was only one way short of murdering his two older brothers to get it. He had to gain their respect. His father had died unexpectedly in June, and here it was the first of November, and Parker and Stephen still hadn't given Adam more responsibility in Garrison, Inc., because they didn't take him seriously. Frustration burned Adam's stomach.

Lauryn's smooth brow furrowed. "I'm confused. I'm Estate's only accountant. How can I get a promotion? Are you planning to hire an assistant for me? Because I assure you, Mr. Garrison, I can handle the workload. I don't need help."

"Adam," he corrected not for the first time. She never relaxed around him. In fact, she always seemed on edge, and he didn't know why. People—women in particular—liked him. More than one reviewer had attributed Estate's popularity to Adam's charm. He knew how to work a crowd, how to make guests feel welcome and want to return.

Of course, he'd never tried to charm Lauryn Lowes. She was an employee and that was a line he'd never crossed. But he would today.

"The president of the Miami Business Council is retiring next year. As you may have heard, it's a pretty conservative group."

She nodded.

"I've been an active member for years, but the council's not willing to entertain the idea of a single guy—especially one who runs a scandalous South Beach nightclub—being in charge no matter how qualified he might be."

"You mean *you* want to run for president?"

The surprise in her voice stung like salt in a fresh wound. "Yes. And the only way for me to have a chance at that nomination is to become the stable, settled guy they require. I won't give up Estate. That means I need to acquire a wife."

Her look of confusion grew. "What does that have to do with me?"

"You're the perfect candidate."

She blinked once, twice, a third time. "To be your *wife?*"

"Yes."

She sat back in the chair, her posture stiffer than usual. After a few moments an uncertain smile wobbled on her lips. "I—I— You're joking. Right?"

Nice lips, he noted. Pale pink. No lipstick. Not collagen enhanced.

Natural. That's it. Lauryn's a natural.

Too bad that would have to change.

"No." He leaned forward and pulled the file pertaining to this merger from the stack on the side of his desk. "Brandon Washington—you've met my attorney—has drawn up the necessary paperwork. I'll pay you five hundred thousand per year for two years plus reasonable living expenses. After that we'll quietly divorce. We'll have a contract and a pre-nuptial agreement. What's yours stays yours including any gifts I buy you. What's mine stays mine."

Extracting the relevant documents, he pushed the pages across the polished wood surface toward her. She didn't take them. "You're welcome to have your attorney look over the agreement."

Tightening her grip on the arms of the chair, she eyed the papers like she would a hungry gator. "You actually expect me to agree to this…proposition?"

"You'll be paid a million dollars to do nothing for two years. Why wouldn't you accept?"

"Because I don't love you?"

A little surprised by her reluctance, he shrugged. He could think of several dozen women who'd jump at this chance, but they weren't the type he needed.

"I don't love you, either, but it's an advantageous match for each of us and a sound business decision. You'll move into my loft and I'll buy you a new car. Maybe a Mercedes or a Volvo wagon. We need to give the impression we'd like to start a family soon."

Eyes wide with shock, she made a choking sound. "A family?"

"We won't of course, but we need to play the part."

"Part?" she echoed.

Lauryn's quick grasp of details was one of the things he'd liked about her at that first interview and in subsequent meetings. But she wasn't picking up quickly now. He stifled his impatience. "The picture of domestic bliss. Stable. Settled. Rooted in the community."

She shook her head as if bewildered. "I'm sorry. I just can't wrap my brain around this. You're seriously asking me to marry you?"

"Yes."

"Mr. Garrison—*Adam*—" Her lips stretched in a fleeting and clearly forced smile. "I'm not the woman for this…position."

"I think you are. You're poised, articulate and conservative. You're exactly what—who—I need, Lauryn."

Although she flushed at his compliments, the words didn't ease the starch from her spine. Biting her bottom lip between straight white teeth, she rose. Her fingers knotted so tightly at her waist that her knuckles gleamed white in the overhead fluorescent light.

"I am extremely flattered by your, um…proposal, but I'm afraid I'll have to decline."

"Lauryn—"

She gasped and worry pleated her brow. "My refusal isn't going to cost me my job, is it?"

"Of course not. What kind of jerk do you think I am? But if you marry me you'll be too busy doing whatever it is South Beach socialites do to put in a forty-hour workweek here."

He came around the desk and stopped just inches from her. For the first time he noticed her scent. She smelled like the night-blooming vines growing on his condo neighbor's patio with an additional kick of something spicy and alluring mixed in. "Consider it a two-year paid vacation. Pampering, shopping—"

"But I enjoy my job. And I like working. I'm sorry, but no thank you. I'm sure you can find someone else who—"

"I don't want anyone else. I want you."

She snapped to attention at his adamant tone and lifted a trembling hand to push her glasses up the bridge of her nose. Adam intercepted, curling his fingers around hers. A spark ignited on contact. He blamed it on the knowledge he was crossing the employee/employer line by touching her and invading her space. Always a risky proposition in this litigious age.

He removed her glasses with his other hand. She had extraordinary eyes. Brighter than olives. Darker than grass. The exact shade of the waters off Miami's coast.

His pulse quickened and his mouth moistened.

Because of what's at stake, he told himself.

He sure as hell wasn't attracted to his mousy bookkeeper. But not being repelled by her was good. Considering…

"I'd be a good husband." His voice came out huskier than

intended. He cleared his throat and continued. "I guarantee you'll be satisfied."

A beat later her eyes widened. "You're saying we'd sleep together?"

"Maybe not sleep. I like my space. I have a study we can convert into a bedroom for you. You'll have privacy when you need it. But for appearances' sake this must appear to be a normal marriage in every way."

"But you'd expect sex. With me." She didn't sound as if she relished the idea and that pricked his pride. He was good in bed, dammit. He'd been perfecting his technique since he was sixteen. And he never left a woman unsatisfied.

"Definitely. We'll be together for two years. That's a long time to be celibate. Infidelity would negate the purpose of the union by showing I couldn't be trusted."

She gaped for a full ten seconds and then yanked her hand free, plucked her glasses from his grasp and backed toward the door. "No. I can't. I won't."

She was turning him down? When had a woman ever turned him down? Hell, when had he ever even had to voice an invitation? Usually he cocked an eyebrow and his choice for the night rushed forward to do whatever he asked. *Whatever* he wanted.

He had to change Lauryn's mind. She was the right woman for the job—an outsider who wouldn't spill all his secrets to the very community of people he was trying to fool. She was smart enough to pull this off, and the timing was too tight for him to search for another candidate. The final slate of business council nominees would be proposed in six months. That meant he needed to prove his stability *now*.

"Name your price, Lauryn."

"I don't have a price. And I think I'd better go."

"I'll call you tomorrow."

"*Don't,* Mr. Garrison. Don't call. Not about…this."

This wasn't going well. "Besides the money, think of the advantages—"

"Of selling my body?"

"—of being my wife. Of being one of the Garrisons of Miami. Doors will open for you."

She gurgled a disgusted sound. "I don't care about getting into A-list nightclubs. I'm not even awake when they're open."

She tilted her head and appraised him through narrowed eyes. The angle revealed the pulse fluttering rapidly at the base of her slender neck. Her ivory skin looked smooth not sun-baked or covered with sprayed-on tan. Was she as pale all over?

"I suppose it's because of your family's wealth and power that you believe you can buy anyone or anything. Like a wife. Or the presidency of the business council."

Damn. "Lauryn—"

She held up a hand. "You should stop now. Before this becomes harassment. Surely your attorney warned you about that?"

Oh yeah. Brandon had warned him in the same breath he'd insisted Lauryn was The One. That warning was the only reason Adam hadn't planted a hot kiss on Lauryn's lips to prove to her that he could please her in bed. But he would never convince her that the marriage could work when she was in this frame of mind. Time for a strategic withdrawal.

"Let me remind you of the confidentiality agreement you signed as part of your employment contract. Anything related to my business, and that includes my strategy to win the Business Council nomination, does not leave this room."

"No one would believe me if I told them Adam Garrison tried to buy a wife. But don't worry. I won't blab unless you make that necessary." She hustled out, closing the door behind her.

Adam shoved a hand through his hair, expelled a frustrated breath and dropped back into his desk chair. He was used to women chasing him—not running from him as if he'd suddenly announced he had the avian flu.

As one of the heirs to the Garrison hospitality and entertainment empire he was a great catch. All the society columns and his tax returns said so. Not only did his family have deep pockets, but Adam's personal investments had exponentially increased his net worth. Add in his recently inherited fifteen percent of Garrison, Inc. and saying he was financially comfortable would be a gross understatement.

And he'd seen a mirror. He wasn't ugly.

So why wasn't Lauryn biting?

There must be something she wanted. Something he could use for leverage.

All he had to do was find it.

The man had to be crazy.

Lauryn placed her purse, car keys and glasses on the kitchen counter of her minuscule apartment and then headed for the bedroom, tugging the pins from her hair as she went.

A marriage of convenience.

What was this? A romance novel? She read them. But she didn't *live* them.

Admittedly, she'd moved to Florida specifically to befriend Adam Garrison.

But she didn't want to *marry* him.

He was a known womanizer who dangled a different celebrity or socialite from his arm almost every night. And with his longish inky dark hair, lady-slayer smile and devastating blue eyes, he invariably chose women equally as gorgeous as himself.

But good looks, she'd learned the hard way, were superficial and sometimes covered an ugly personality. They definitely attracted the wrong kinds of attention, which was why she'd quit flaunting her curves and started dressing to fade into the background.

She removed her suit, returned it to the hanger, toed off her pumps and placed them on the shoe rack.

"Huh. He says he likes his space, but I'll bet he never goes to bed alone," she muttered to herself as she pulled on a pair of faded sweats and an old T-shirt of her father's. "He probably serves his women's orgasms with a cab fare chaser."

As an accountant she couldn't help but consider all she could accomplish with a million dollars, starting with replenishing the bank account she'd depleted to move cross country and take a job with Adam's club—a job she'd specifically targeted when her research revealed he was the new deedholder to her family's estate.

But marriage? No way. She'd had one disastrous marriage that began for all the wrong reasons. It wasn't an experience she ever intended repeating.

Not even as a business deal.

A very lucrative business deal.

Forget it.

She padded barefoot to the kitchen, withdrew last night's Chinese takeout leftovers and popped them in the microwave. The scent of Hunan shrimp mingled with citrus in the air as she peeled an orange to go with her dinner.

If you lived with him you'd get to know him well.

Well enough to convince him let her pry up a few closet floorboards in the fifteen-million-dollar estate he'd bought eighteen months ago?

Why had he spent a fortune on a house if he wasn't going to live there? She'd thought maybe he intended to remodel first, but a check at the courthouse revealed no building permits had been issued prior to her arrival, and as far as she could tell with her frequent drive-bys nothing beyond routine maintenance had been done to the house since her move to Florida.

A lawn-care company groomed the lush yard, and she'd seen a pool-service company's van in the circular driveway. She thought she'd spotted tennis courts on the other side of the stone and wrought iron fence but the bougainvillea hedge was too thick to be certain, and the exclusive Sunset Island wasn't exactly the kind of neighborhood where you could climb fences to peer over the top without getting arrested.

The estate wasn't within walking distance of the club like Adam's condo, but even in heavy traffic and with all the South Beach road construction the commute would take less than twenty minutes.

While the food heated she set the table. Her mother—her heart hitched—her *adoptive* mother, she corrected, had always made a big production of setting the table. It was one of the many things she and Lauryn had done together. All that had changed eleven months ago when Lauryn's father died and her "mother" had shared the letters.

Letters that had been locked in a safety-deposit box for decades.

Letters from her father's former lover.

Letters that had upended Lauryn's life and sent her on a three-thousand-mile quest to find the woman who'd loved her enough to have her but not enough to keep her.

Adrianna Laurence.

Her birthmother.

How could her father have lied? Lauryn asked herself for the billionth time. And how could her mother have let him?

The timer beeped. On autopilot Lauryn retrieved the carton, scraped the contents onto a plate and pulled a Diet Coke with lime from the fridge.

Hadn't her father realized what a shock it would be for Lauryn to suddenly discover she wasn't who she'd thought she was for the past twenty-six years?

Hadn't he known finding out she was the by-product of her father's affair with a Miami Beach socialite would make Lauryn doubt everything she'd once held as truth?

Why hadn't he guessed that finding out he'd married his deceased buddy's pregnant wife only to provide a mother for his infant daughter would make Lauryn question the very fabric of her parents' marriage? Or that discovering the child growing in her "mother's" rounded tummy in all those pictures wasn't Lauryn at all, but a baby boy who had died before taking his first breath?

Why couldn't her father have told her about her birthmother earlier? Before Adrianna had died. If he'd done so Lauryn would have had a chance to meet the woman who'd given her life and ask questions. She could have heard her mother's voice, seen her face and learned about her parents' relationship. What attracted them? What separated them? What had driven Adrianna to give her baby away and why had she died so young?

Even Lauryn's name was part of the mystery. *Laur*ence. *Laur*yn. According to Lauryn's adoptive mother, Adrianna Laurence had insisted on the name. Was it because she wanted Lauryn to find her one day? Or because she couldn't bear not being a part of her daughter's life in some small way?

Lauryn might never discover the reason, but it wouldn't be from lack of trying on her part.

If her father had told the truth then Lauryn wouldn't be forced to use subterfuge to find her answers.

Answers that, according to the letters, might be found in a diary hidden in a secret compartment beneath the closet floorboards of the estate Adam Garrison now owned.

Were the diaries still there? Or had someone besides her mother known about them and removed them from their hiding place long ago? From Lauryn's research she knew that her grandmother, the last surviving member of the Laurence clan, had died shortly before Adam bought the property.

Doors will open for you, Adam had said.

The only doors Lauryn wanted to open were the ones to that house. Her birthmother's house. But she couldn't just blurt out her odd request. If she did and Adam turned her down, then she'd have nowhere else to turn, and she'd never have her questions answered.

And so the deceit began. She'd moved from California to Florida planning to befriend her new boss and gain his trust. She'd believed that once she did that, once she'd proven she wasn't some flake with outlandish ideas, he'd be more likely to grant her bizarre request to pry up a few floorboards.

Only it hadn't worked out the way she'd hoped. She and Adam only saw each other in a business setting at biweekly meetings. There was nothing remotely personal in discussing the club's bottom line and there were always other employees in the vicinity.

And now…

She stared at her steaming dinner with absolutely no appetite.

Now, Adam's crazy plan and her refusal to participate in it had probably ruined any chance of friendship or trust ever developing. She'd be lucky if she escaped this situation with her job.

She'd have to find a way—short of marriage—to make amends or kiss her quest for answers goodbye.

Two

Getting out of the building for an hour on Friday appealed to Lauryn about as much as winning the lottery.

With the club operating from 11:00 p.m. to 5:00 a.m., Adam didn't usually make appearances in the Estate offices until late afternoon. While he slept, a hive of office staff, custodians and food and beverage restockers did their jobs to prepare for the night ahead. Nevertheless, Lauryn had jumped at every sound this morning and looked forward to taking the bus to her favorite Dolphin Mall deli and spending a relaxing hour not worrying about Adam Garrison's bizarre proposition.

The clock ticked noon. *Time to escape.* Tension drained from her knotted shoulders. She pulled her purse from her desk and took her usual circuit through the club. With the lights turned low, the antebellum structure that had begun life as a French-owned casino looked as if it, too, were sleeping.

Later this afternoon the building would awaken as the technicians tested every speaker and bulb and set up whatever stage requirements tonight's entertainers demanded.

The club was designed around a "night out at home" theme, and each room in the vast building had been set up with trendy leather sofas and chairs arranged in conversational nooks. There were multiple bars and dance floors on both levels, each having its own color scheme. State-of-the-art lighting and sound systems and top-notch live entertainment kept the place packed to its twenty-five-hundred-person capacity with an A-list crowd every night. Or so she'd heard. She hadn't been a customer yet and probably never would be since she'd given up late-night partying years ago and she didn't fit the guest profile.

She paused to caress the carved newel post of the grand staircase sweeping up to the second floor. This was her favorite part of Estate. She'd always thought it resembled a stage from a Hollywood movie set.

Thinking of Hollywood reminded her of California and home.

Home. And the mother she'd inadvertently hurt when Susan Lowes had revealed Lauryn's true parentage.

Way to go, Lauryn. Shoot the messenger.

Lauryn hadn't meant to imply Susan had been anything less than a perfect mother. But Lauryn had questions about her heritage. Questions Susan couldn't answer. And then there was the anger. Anger toward her father and Susan for withholding the truth. Anger toward Lauryn's birthmother for rejecting her without even giving her a chance to fit into her world.

Shaking off her unproductive emotions, Lauryn circled back toward the employee exit, shoved open the side door and stepped into the Miami sunshine and balmy November day.

The first thing she saw once her eyes adjusted to the brightness was Adam Garrison leaning against a silver BMW convertible parked by the curb.

Her stomach dropped like a cruise ship anchor and her nerves knotted like a snarled line. So much for avoiding him after yesterday's fiasco. She hoped he wasn't waiting for her.

Reluctantly, she made her way down the sidewalk. She had to walk past him to get to the bus stop a block away. Lauryn had quickly learned that driving in South Beach was a disaster, not due to the traffic but because of the parking. Specifically, the lack thereof. So she relied on the bus system to get to and from work most of the time.

"Good afternoon, Lauryn." Adam straightened as she neared.

At several inches over six feet, he looked lean and athletic in sharply creased chocolate slacks that accentuated his height and a cream silk T-shirt that emphasized the breadth of his shoulders. A breeze ruffled his dark hair, which always looked in need of a trim. She'd bet he paid a fortune for that casually unkempt look. Thankfully, his designer sunglasses covered his gorgeous make-Jell-O-of-her-kneecaps blue eyes.

She was ashamed to admit that in the beginning she'd had a bit of a crush on her boss, but then stories of his swinging bachelor lifestyle and short attention span with women had eroded those feelings. She'd been there, done that and didn't ever want to live that kind of superficial, self-absorbed life again.

Adam was gorgeous, but good-looking men were a dime a dozen in South Beach. Not that she was shopping for one. You couldn't walk down the sidewalk without passing a barechested guy showing off his tan and pecs—either of which may or may not be real here in a city where artificial beauty was as common as a cold.

But most of those guys didn't make her pulse blip unevenly.

And none of them had proposed.

"Good afternoon, Mr.—Adam. Did you need me for something?"

Please say no.

"Lunch."

Not the answer she wanted. "I…have plans."

He frowned. "A date?"

She hesitated and debated lying. But she couldn't. Her presence in Miami was already complicated by too many half-truths. "No. I was going to the mall."

"I have a better idea. Get in." He opened the passenger-side door.

Would he fire her if she refused? Not something she wanted to find out. She eased into the leather seat and fastened her safety belt. Adam slid into the driver's seat, started the engine and merged into the Washington Avenue traffic.

"I only have an hour," she reminded him.

"Not a problem. Besides, you're with the boss. Who's going to report you?" He drove north for a couple of miles and then cut through to North Bay and turned back south. Seconds later he pulled up to the curb in front of an exclusive restaurant overlooking Biscayne Bay—one she'd never been to because A, she couldn't afford it, and B, she couldn't get a reservation even if she wanted one.

He climbed from the car and tossed the keys to the valet. Another uniformed employee opened Lauryn's door, handed her out and escorted her to Adam waiting on the sidewalk as if she were a prized possession. Or a ditz who couldn't be trusted next to the busy street.

"Good afternoon, Mr. Garrison," the hostess greeted him

the second they stepped through the doors. Her cool gaze assessed and dismissed Lauryn in two seconds flat. "Your table is ready."

Adam motioned for Lauryn to precede him, but then followed so closely she could feel his heat and his gaze on her back. She hoped her pin-striped navy skirt didn't make her butt look big. And then she mentally kicked herself.

His opinion of your butt is irrelevant.

Conscious of the curious stares and her department-store clothing so different from the rest of the clientele's designer wear, Lauryn followed the hostess to a waterfront table on the outside deck, took a seat beneath the umbrella and accepted a menu. A breeze teased strands of her hair from the knot at her nape to tickle her cheeks.

She looked up and directly into Adam's blue eyes. He'd removed his sunglasses. As always, the intensity and intelligence in his gaze made her breath hitch.

Tension invaded her limbs as she waited for him to bring up the proposal because there was no doubt that's why he'd brought her here. She hadn't changed her mind about marrying him, although the idea had monopolized her thoughts and cost her a decent night's sleep. Lunch at an exclusive restaurant wouldn't sway her.

What kind of man coolly plotted to buy a wife, sleep with her for two years even though he didn't love her and then discard her and walk away? But then Adam probably hadn't loved any of the women who'd creased his sheets.

Having been burned by love, Lauryn could see the advantages of avoiding the unpredictable emotion, but call her a romantic sap; she actually wanted to find her soul mate one day.

She ducked her head and fussed with her napkin. She'd thought her parents had been soul mates, but discovering the letters and the lies had made her question every tender gesture she'd witnessed over the years. What had been real? What had been staged? Had they fallen for each other after the convoluted coverup of Lauryn's adoption and the premature death of Susan's baby like Susan claimed? Or was that also a lie?

After the waiter took their orders Adam gave Lauryn his full attention. His gaze roamed her features as if cataloging each one. "You moved here from California. Which part?"

Small talk. She could do small talk. Although it had been so long since she'd been on a date she was probably rusty. Was this a date? She hoped not. "Northern."

"Why Florida?"

She'd had enough doors slammed in her face to know she certainly couldn't blurt out the whole truth. Adam belonged to the same upper class who'd closed ranks and shut her out when she'd come here ten months ago to ask questions about one of their own. No one would confirm that Adrianna had given birth to an illegitimate child, and no one would tell Lauryn how her birthmother died. In fact, conversations ended pretty quickly as soon as she mentioned Adrianna Laurence's name.

Adrianna's obituary hadn't listed a cause of death or even an organization to which one could donate in lieu of flowers as a clue. She'd only been thirty-six, ten years older than Lauryn was now. If there was a ticking time bomb in Lauryn's genes she would like to know.

"My father used to be stationed at Tyndall Air Force Base. I grew up hearing stories about Florida, the Everglades and the beaches. After he died I decided to check them out for myself."

"And yet you settled on the east coast rather than panhandle."

"Better job opportunities," she replied and hoped he'd drop the subject. He'd been the only job opportunity she'd pursued, and she considered it an amazing stroke of luck that his previous accountant had quit to stay at home with her new baby around the same time Lauryn had needed her job.

"California's loss is my gain." He accompanied the words with a smile she'd only seen in the South Florida Album section of the newspaper, but those grainy pictures in no way had the same lung-emptying impact as the real deal. No wonder flocks of women fell at his feet. She felt almost dizzy.

She transferred her gaze to the islands across the bay. The Sunset Islands were a tiny cluster of outrageously priced real estate. Could you see Adam's other home—her birth-mother's family estate—from here? She counted until she found the correct channel to mark the way to the waterfront property. Lauryn had considered renting a boat and trying to get a better view of the house from the bay side, but the only thing she knew about boats was that they made her seasick.

The man in front of her held the answers. "Didn't I hear someone say you own a house on one of those islands?"

Adam nodded. "Ricco?"

What did the club's booking agent have to do with the estate? But he wasn't her source. She'd discovered that tidbit during a search of the county records, but if she told Adam that she'd come across as a stalker. Which she was…sort of. And she didn't want to get Ricco in trouble. "I don't remember."

"I bought the house at auction the same way I bought the building now housing Estate and a few other properties. Bargain prices. Good investments."

"And yet you don't live on the island."

"I use the Sunset estate to house certain VIPs who are performing at the club. The ones who prefer privacy to hotels."

That explained the maintenance crews. "I didn't know that."

He reached across the table and covered her hand with his. A zing shot up her arm—the same kind of tempting tingle she'd experienced yesterday when he'd held her hand. Lauryn was no stranger to sexual attraction, but she'd learned the hard way to ignore it because sex inevitably led to complications. Complications she didn't need.

She tried to pull away, but Adam's grip tightened around her wrist. He turned her hand over, used his other hand to pry open her clenched fist and then drew on her palm with his fingertip. The impact hit her libido like a car bomb. Shockwaves plowed through her and shattered defenses she'd thought unbreakable. She gulped and squeezed her knees against the warmth gathering between her thighs.

"I apologize for springing my proposal on you so abruptly yesterday. I realize it's a pretty radical idea."

"No kidding," she croaked and tugged her hand to no avail.

"You don't know me well enough to know I always give one hundred ten percent to any endeavor. I can and will be a great husband." He stroked up and down between each of her fingers. Her pulse bounded like popcorn in a popper. No doubt he felt it beneath the thumb he feathered over the inside of her wrist. "We'll get to know each other better. Date a few times."

"I—I don't think that's a good idea. And it won't change my answer."

"You can't deny there's chemistry between us."

His deep, velvety tone immediately made her think of

dark nights, tangled sheets, a lack of clothing and his hands on her skin.

Heat flushed her from the inside out. How long had it been since she'd had really good sex? Or sex, period, for that matter.

Did he really feel the attraction, too, or was he just saying what he needed to say to close this deal? God knows she'd fallen victim to plenty of smooth-talking guys who'd made her feel like the most important person on the planet until they had what they wanted. But then she'd been known to use guys, too, to get a rise out of her father.

She scanned Adam's face, noting the dusky color on his cheekbones and the way he breathed through slightly parted lips.

Adam Garrison attracted to *her?* Impossible. She'd seen his usual bimbos and she didn't even come close to the models and starlets he dated, especially the way she dressed these days.

"You're my boss. Office relationships always turn out badly—usually for the employee."

"They don't have to. Besides, you won't be working for me after the wedding," he enunciated very clearly and a tad too loud. Before she could figure out why he'd spoken that way a woman jerked to a halt behind him.

"Adam?" The lady could have been anywhere from fifty to a well-preserved seventy, but it was impossible to gauge by her tightly stretched skin.

Adam looked up and hesitated just the right amount of time before releasing Lauryn's hand and standing. "Good afternoon, Mrs. Ainsley. This is Lauryn Lowes. Lauryn, Helene Ainsley. She's on the board of practically every charitable foundation in Miami."

Helene Ainsley. The same woman who'd refused to come

to the door when Lauryn had knocked and asked the maid who answered for a moment of her mistress's time. The Ainsley estate was four doors down from the Laurence property, and even though Mrs. Ainsley was older, she or her children had probably known Adrianna Laurence.

"It's nice to meet you, Mrs. Ainsley." It would have been nicer ten months ago.

The woman looked from Adam to Lauryn through her nipped and tucked eyes. "Do we have news?"

Lauryn tensed and held her breath.

Adam sent a lingering look her way and then smiled tenderly before replying without breaking eye contact, "No news."

Good grief, the man should be an actor. His tone, expression and body language spoke the opposite more eloquently than words.

"I could have sworn I heard you say 'wedding.'"

Adam returned his attention to Mrs. Ainsley. "You could have. There have been a few weddings in the Garrison family lately. And of course, my sister Brittany is engaged."

But Mrs. Ainsley didn't believe him. Lauryn could see the curiosity in the woman's overstretched face. How smart of Adam to plant the seed—just in case he convinced Lauryn to say yes. Not that he would.

The woman's searching gaze focused on Lauryn. "Have we met, dear? You look familiar."

Lauryn's heart skipped a beat. Did she take after her mother? The only photos she'd found of Adrianna had been blurry black-and-white newspaper shots that made identifying specific features difficult, but Lauryn had inherited her father's coloring. Her mother had been a brunette. "No, ma'am."

"Are you quite sure? I never forget a face."

She yearned to blurt out the truth, but the consequences of handling this badly were too great. "I'm sure. I haven't met many people because I haven't lived in the area very long."

"Then we should remedy that. We're having a few friends over on Saturday. Perhaps you and Adam will join us for couples' tennis?"

The invitation stole Lauryn's breath.

Doors will open, Adam had said. Lauryn hadn't considered that those open doors would offer an opportunity to join her birthmother's social circle.

If she married Adam Garrison she'd be one of the Miami elite and closer to getting her answers than ever before. The idea tempted her more than it should.

"Lauryn?" he asked.

"I, um…I'm sorry. I don't play tennis." She'd been too busy being a rebellious teen to learn. Just one more reason to regret her misspent youth.

Helene turned back to Adam. "Then perhaps you'll bring Lauryn to cocktails on Monday evening. The club is closed then, isn't it?"

"We'd like that," Adam accepted without consulting Lauryn. But she didn't care about his high-handedness. He was going to get her into a house her mother had probably visited and introduce her to people her mother had probably known. While they were on the island maybe she could convince him to show her his place and she could walk her mother's path.

"Lovely. See you at eight." Mrs. Ainsley glided off with the grace of the queen.

Adam sat quickly, followed by the arrival of their meal. After the waiter departed Lauryn looked at her companion. "You're very sneaky."

A mischievous smile slanted his lips, making him look like

a bad boy inviting her to come out and play. The dormant rebel in Lauryn raised its head, but she quickly reined in her naughty urges. She'd given up her penchant for bad boys.

"I know what I want and I'm not ashamed to go after it. Helene is one of the biggest gossips in the Greater Miami area. By the time we announce our engagement it will be old news."

She gaped at him. "Need I remind you that I turned you down?"

"You'll change your mind." He lifted his wineglass in a silent toast. His eyes held a challenge. "Or I'll change it for you. We'll be good together, Lauryn. In bed and out."

Tendrils of desire wound through her. And that, Lauryn realized, was the crux of her dilemma. The answers she wanted were right at her fingertips, but only if she broke the promise she'd made to her father and herself before the ink on her annulment had dried.

Next time, she'd vowed, she'd marry for all the right reasons.

And the business alliance Adam proposed didn't even come close.

He almost had her.

Adam didn't know why the idea of drinks with the Ainsleys' stuffy crowd excited Lauryn, but he'd seen the flash of interest in her eyes and the heightened color on her cheeks earlier at lunch.

He rinsed the last of the shaving cream from his face, patted dry and then padded naked into his bedroom to dress for a Friday night at the club. He fed off the pulse of the music, the flash of the lights and the energy of Estate's guests. Knowing he provided a good time for hundreds of people each night and was financially rewarded for doing so filled him with satisfaction.

Work. He lived for it. Why couldn't his family—specifically his brothers—see that? But they viewed his life as one big party and treated him like a perpetual frat boy.

He made it halfway across the room before the mental image of Lauryn in his bed stalled his steps. Hell, he couldn't be attracted to her, could he? Before Brandon's suggestion, Adam had never had a sexual thought about his accountant. Or any employee, for that matter.

Lauryn had done nothing to light his fire. She was cool and withdrawn. She didn't flirt. Even though he'd spent an hour with her today, he didn't know any more about her than he had before lunch except that the smiles he used to make other women melt didn't affect Lauryn Lowes.

But he had to admit something happened when he touched her to quicken his pulse and heat his blood. Was his interest piqued solely because she'd said no?

Shaking his head to clear the image of her pale skin spread across his black sheets, he headed for his closet. Any anticipation he might feel for seeing her again could be attributed to moving closer toward his goal. The marriage would be strictly business. Not pleasure. Although he was beginning to suspect Lauryn had a good body beneath her shapeless clothing and that he could derive a great deal of pleasure from exploring it.

All right, so he wanted to see her naked, but that was only because he was curious to know what she was hiding and why.

And if she wanted to dip her toes in Miami Beach society, he'd lead her to the water even though he usually avoided such events like he'd avoid swimming through a school of jellyfish. You never knew when you might get stung.

Drinks at the Ainsleys' could include anywhere from a half-dozen to a hundred guests. Adam hoped like hell his mother wouldn't be there drinking herself into oblivion. Lauryn would get a dose of Bonita Garrison soon enough.

After the wedding he and Lauryn would have to attend some of the Sunday family dinners, but until then he didn't dare risk letting his mother's increasingly bitter barbs scare off Lauryn because he didn't have the time or inclination to search out another wife candidate. The nominating committee had already begun their search.

Guilt nagged at Adam as he dragged on a silk shirt. Finding out her husband of thirty-eight years had a twenty-seven-year-old illegitimate daughter from a long-term and on-going affair couldn't have been easy for his mother. But that was no excuse for pickling her liver by living in a bottle of booze. His mother's drinking had been a problem for as long as Adam could remember, and with it came the lies and excuses to cover the things she'd done or forgotten to do. But the situation had worsened since the reading of the will and the open acknowledgment of Cassie, his father's illegitimate daughter by his Bahamian lover.

Adam made a note to hire a full-time driver for his mother. He couldn't risk letting her get behind the wheel of a car. And he needed to talk to his siblings about drying her out before she killed herself.

He stepped into his trousers and pulled them over his bare butt. He hadn't known about his halfsister, Cassie, but he had known about his father's affair for years. Should he have told his mother? Or had she already known? Was that why she drank?

Five years ago during a trip to the Bahamas, Adam had stumbled upon his father and Cassie's mother in an intimate clench. He'd tried to force his father to end the affair and failed. The confrontation had been ugly. Later that same year his father had turned over the running of Garrison, Inc. to

Parker and the hotel operations to Stephen. Adam had received nothing. Nada.

And now it was too late to make things right with his father.

He tamped down the loss and frustration tightening his chest and finished dressing, then grabbed his keys and cell phone and jogged down the stairs. He couldn't go backward. He could only move forward.

For his plan to work he needed absolute secrecy. Only Brandon knew the whole truth behind Adam's proposal. And even though his best friend was crazy in love with Adam's newly discovered half sister, Adam knew he could count on Brandon to keep his lips zipped. Not just because of client confidentiality, but because Brandon was that kind of guy—as honest and loyal as a summer day is long.

In the meantime, Adam would keep Lauryn away from his family until the contracts were signed and the wedding knot was tightly tied—and he had no doubt it would be tied. If Lauryn slipped up and revealed his strategy to his siblings he wouldn't have a chance in hell of gaining more involvement in Garrison, Inc.

But first he had to get through Monday evening. A night at the Ainsleys' wouldn't be pleasant, but neither would it be a total waste of time. With Lauryn on his arm he'd schmooze with the movers and shakers of the community who could aid in his quest for the council nomination.

A win-win situation.

He'd score points with Lauryn and for himself.

And he'd do what he did best.

He'd turn on the charm and land himself a bride.

Three

Yet another dead end.

Lauryn tried to keep her steps from dragging as she followed Adam into the moist evening air and across the brick courtyard toward his car. She'd pinned her hopes on walking in her birthmother's footsteps tonight. But Adrianna Laurence had never set foot in the Ainsleys' house. At least, not this one.

Lauryn's disappointment was almost enough to distract her from the feel of Adam's hand wrapped around hers. Hot. Firm. Electric.

He'd been attentive all evening with a casual touch at her waist here, a brush of his hand against hers there. It hadn't taken her long to realize his every move had been designed to convince the other guests they were a couple. And yet he hadn't said one dishonest word or made a single inappropriate gesture to which she could object.

Much as she disliked the situation, she had to face facts.
Being a pawn in Adam's scheme had its benefits. She'd been
the only outsider at the gathering tonight, but because she was
Adam's date she'd been welcomed into her birthmother's
stratum by the same people who'd refused to speak to her a few
months ago. People who had very likely known her birthmother.

With a little Garrison grease to oil the hinges she'd made
more progress tonight in two hours of chitchat than she had
in weeks of knocking on doors and researching microfiche
newspaper articles and county documents. She didn't have
her answers yet because it was too soon to ask without risking
rejection, but as long as she was beside Adam she could
build the tentative connections to find out what she wanted
so desperately to know.

Adam opened the car door, but Lauryn didn't climb in. She
pivoted in her flat sandals and studied the ostentatious home.
Lights streamed from every window, painting stripes across
the dark grounds. "You're telling me the Ainsleys demolished
a perfectly good house and built a new one in the same spot?"

"Five years ago."

"But why?" She turned back to Adam and realized he'd
moved close enough to loom above her—far too close for her
peace of mind. The tang of his cologne, a crisp lime scent,
teased her senses, and she could see the fine lines at the
corners of his eyes. Her body still hummed from his unexpected touches throughout the evening and his proximity
overwhelmed her.

One small step and they'd be breast-to-chest, hip-to-hip.
Her gaze drifted to his lips. With all the practice he'd had,
she'd bet he was a great kisser. If he bent his head—

No kisses. Back up.

But she couldn't. Trapped as she was between the car and

Adam's lean frame, there was nowhere to run. She forced her eyes away from his mouth and dragged a lungful of the heavily scented night air into her chest, but she couldn't identify the flowers she smelled.

Had her mother known the names? Had Adrianna been a plant lover? A swimmer? A shopaholic? A night owl or morning person? Tall, short, introvert or extrovert? Had she been a rule follower or a rule breaker? Knowing nothing frustrated Lauryn and left her feeling empty. Adrift.

Adam shrugged. "With the shortage of land and surplus of cash in South Florida it's a common practice to tear down and start fresh. Sometimes massive reconstruction is due to hurricane damage, but in this case Helene wanted renovations that exceeded the value of the house."

Alarm streaked through her. "Your house hasn't been razed has it?"

His eyes narrowed as if he could hear the panic she couldn't quite keep out of her voice. "No. It's the original structure. Why?"

Get a grip, Lauryn. She forced a smile. "I…um, love history. I hate to see it erased. We're close to your place, aren't we? Would you show it to me?"

He hesitated so long she thought he'd refuse. "Sure. There's no one staying there this week."

She slid into the car with so much anticipation and excitement bubbling through her veins that she could barely sit still.

Adam drove off the Ainsley property, down the palm-shadowed street and then pulled into a short driveway blocked by another set of elaborately coiled iron gates and stopped the car. He tapped a security code onto a recessed keypad and the wide gates silently glided open.

Emotion clogged Lauryn's throat as the car rolled into a circular brick courtyard and around the center fountain.

Sensor lights flicked on, flooding the area with light. Scrambling to absorb it all at once, she ticked off details in her mind. Mediterranean style. Four-car garage to the left. Arched windows. Carved columns. Deep, shadowed porches.

Her birthmother's home. Lauryn's heart thumped as hard and fast as a helicopter's blades as she climbed from the car on trembling legs. She wished she could see the house in daylight instead of washed by a weak crescent moon. She wanted to examine every minute detail of the elaborately carved cornices above the windows and doors and under the gables and eaves.

"It's beautiful," she whispered.

"Like I said, it's a good investment. By the time I unload it, the property will have doubled in value."

Panic burst in her veins. He couldn't sell. Not yet. "You're going to sell it?"

"When the market and price are right."

She wiped her dampening palms on her simple black sheath and followed Adam onto the front porch, tangling and untangling her fingers while he unlocked the door.

How many times had her birthmother crossed this threshold?

He entered, hit a light switch and then punched a sequence on an alarm system concealed by a small mirror. He gestured for her to join him, but she couldn't move. A weird form of near-paralysis locked her muscles. She was so close to uncovering the truth. So close to the diaries and answers.

If they were here.

But what if she didn't like what she learned? What if her mother wasn't a nice person? What if her mother had died of some hideously debilitating and hereditary disease? And what if Lauryn possessed some flaw that made her unlovable?

Her father and Susan had loved her hadn't they? Maybe. Her parents had lied about so much that Lauryn didn't trust herself to recognize the truth anymore.

"Lauryn?" Adam's expression asked why she delayed.

She scrambled for a response. "This luxury is about as far as you can get from the military housing I grew up in."

"Didn't seem to bother you at the Ainsleys'."

"I guess I was too nervous about meeting all those people to be overwhelmed by the house. I, um…don't get out much." Not anymore.

She forced her feet forward and found herself in a soaring circular two-story domed foyer. She slowly turned around in the center of the Mariner's Compass pattern inlaid into the marble floor like a glossy stone quilt, and then crossed to the wide staircase sweeping up and around the foyer to the second floor.

Had her mother crept up and down these stairs, avoiding the squeaky treads in the middle of the night? If marble treads creaked, that is.

Had the wild streak that had landed Lauryn in so much trouble as a teen come from Adrianna Laurence? Lauryn certainly hadn't inherited it from her father, a regimented career military man, or learned it from her adoptive mother, a serene saint of a woman who never raised her voice or her hand no matter how obnoxious Lauryn had been.

"Want the ten-dollar tour?" Adam's voice intruded.

She blinked. "I thought that was a ten-cent tour."

"Inflation," Adam replied straight-faced. "If you don't have cash, I'll accept a more creative payment."

His gaze dropped to Lauryn's lips and her mouth dried. She cleared her throat and looked away. "I'd love a tour."

She had to get into this house without him dogging her footsteps. Maybe she could convince him to give her a key to drop stuff off for the VIPs and steal a few minutes to explore. "How many bedrooms?"

"Six bedrooms, seven and a half baths, plus servants' apartments over the garage."

Six! It would take hours or days to search each closet for loose floorboards and that was assuming the closets were empty and she wouldn't have to shift stuff out of the way first.

"This is definitely the kind of house to raise a family in." Her mother had grown up here, an only child, and according to what little Lauryn had uncovered, had moved back home after one semester at Vassar. Had Adrianna taken the diaries to college with her? Had she brought them home?

"Come on." He turned and headed through an archway.

Lauryn hustled after him. "Did you make many changes after you bought the estate?"

He strode past a stream of rooms, flipping light switches as he went. "Other than updating the electrical wiring, no. The previous owners kept the place well-maintained. I even bought some of the furniture in the estate sale."

Lauryn stumbled. She barely caught a glimpse of the book-lined library, home theater, massive kitchen, two-story living room and beamed-ceiling den as she hustled to keep up with Adam. The grandeur of the house blew her mind. She wanted to beg him to slow down, to let her soak up the details like a sponge, to ask which pieces of furniture had been the Laurences'.

Had her mother sat on that sofa or at that writing desk? But asking would require explanations. And explanations could lead to rejection. It was too soon to launch her appeal.

He didn't stop until he reached a circular sunroom jutting from the back of the house like a peninsula. Three of her tiny apartments would fit in this room alone.

To her right a wall of windows overlooked an expansive

pool and patio illuminated by subtle landscape lighting. The left side revealed tennis courts, and beyond the seawall at the back of the property stretched a private dock with a long, low and fast-looking boat floating in the channel.

With one sweep of his hand Adam extinguished the interior and exterior lights and the outside view vanished. Pale moonlight cast the sunroom in a mysterious combination of shadows and wavering silvery light.

"Ready to go?"

No! Not yet. "You're not going to show me the upstairs?"

He closed the distance between them in two lazy strides, lifted his hand and cupped her cheek. Surprise held her motionless. Shadows sharpened the angles of his face. His thumb brushed over her lips. Desire sparked instantly in her veins and judging by the sudden widening of Adam's pupils and the flare of his nostrils he felt something, too. The air suddenly turned hot, humid and heavy.

"If you want to get me into a bedroom, you're going to have to accept my proposal and sign the agreements first."

Her thoughts screeched to a halt. She could not let herself fall for Adam Garrison. She'd given up bad boys and shallow relationships a long time ago. And while Adam wore designer clothing instead of torn jeans, he was still a heartbreaker through and through.

Been there. Done that.

Tempting, but taboo.

But she had to have access to this house. She'd lost her father and her own identity eleven months ago and possibly shattered her relationship with her mother beyond repair. If she had any chance of getting her life back on an even keel then she had to figure out who she was—who she *really* was—not the fairy tale her parents had concocted.

There was only one way.

A chill raced through her. She spun away from Adam, wrapped her arms around herself and picked her way through the mottled shadows to stand by the window and stare out at the lights winking across the darkness from the houses on the island across the channel.

"I'll do it," she said in a rush with her gaze focused on the rocking boat instead of the man behind her.

Light filled the room once again. "Do what?"

She slowly turned and met Adam's direct gaze. "I'll marry you. But only if we live here."

"I have a condo within walking distance of the club."

"Have you ever considered you might appear more settled if you lived in a house instead of a bachelor pad?"

He dipped his head. "Good point."

"I won't give up my job."

"Lauryn, you won't need to work."

"But I want to." She took a slow breath and then blurted, "And I won't sleep with you."

"You'll have your own room."

"No, Adam, I mean no sex. You might be able to be intimate with someone you don't love, but I can't." Not anymore. She remembered all too well the self-loathing afterward. She'd wanted to hurt her father with her brazen behavior, but she'd only ended up hurting and hating herself.

"I'll get tested if that's what you're worried about."

"That has nothing to do with it. I mean, it is important given the legions you're rumored to have bedded, but—"

"Legions?"

"You're not known for your discriminatory tastes."

"There haven't been legions."

"How many then?"

"None of your business."

"It is when you're trying to talk me into bed."

He hesitated and then shrugged. "I don't know."

"You didn't count or you can't count that high?"

His chin jutted forward. "How many men have you slept with?"

Her shameful past crept over her. She'd wasted her youth looking for ways to flout her father's iron-fist authority, and she wasn't proud of that. She'd been a rebel, but she'd reformed. She'd practically become a nun. "Hey, if you don't have to answer then neither do I."

"What am I supposed to do for…relief?"

A slideshow flashed in her mind of ten different ways she could give him sexual relief, but she shut it down. The heat flushing her skin wasn't as easy to vanquish. "That depends on whether you're right- or left-handed."

"And you?"

Her cheeks ignited. "I can take care of myself."

His jaw muscles bunched as if he were gritting his teeth. He paced to the window, paused and then turned. "Fine. I accept your terms. Do you have a passport?"

For a moment she was too stunned to speak. "Yes. Why?"

"I'll have Brandon make the arrangements. He and Cassie can set up a quick, quiet Bahamas wedding. Does that suit you? Or do you need a circus?"

Cassie…it took a moment for Lauryn to place the name. Cassie Sinclair had been John Garrison's secret lovechild from an extramarital affair. Or so the papers reported. Even though Lauryn had never met the woman, she felt a kinship with her. Another outsider. But at least Cassie had known who her parents were. Cassie currently owned and managed the Garrison Grand-Bahamas and had recently hooked up with Brandon Washington, Adam's attorney—if the club's scuttlebutt was to be believed.

"I don't want a big wedding. But why the Bahamas?"

"If we get married in Miami my family would expect to be invited and there's a good chance there would be a media blitz."

Avoiding both the media and the Garrison family appealed. "Something quiet in the Bahamas is fine. I've never been there."

"We'll stay a few days and call it a honeymoon."

Honeymoon? "I won't change my mind about the sex."

"Lauryn, it's imperative we act like a couple who's fallen in love and eloped. If this marriage doesn't look real it'll do me no good. We'll have a honeymoon."

"The business council nomination is that important to you?"

Again he hesitated. "It's what the nomination represents that's important."

"And that is?"

"Personal." He glanced at his watch. "If we leave now we have time to swing by the club and pick up the agreements."

Personal.

Secrets weren't the best way to start a marriage—temporary or otherwise. But she'd let him get away with this one because she had a few of her own.

Some things were too shameful to share.

"You didn't have to drive me home," Lauryn said as Adam turned his BMW into her apartment complex.

"I told you I'm not letting you take the bus at this time of night."

"I always use the bus."

"Not anymore. My fiancée would never use public transportation."

Fiancée. She gulped down her rising panic. Her last marriage had been a horrific mistake. Would this one be better or worse since love wasn't involved?

"Your fiancée can't afford valet parking or dollar-an-hour parking meters."

"With the money you're about to receive that's going to change."

As bad luck would have it, one of the few visitors' parking spaces opened up as he turned into the lot. He pulled between the white lines, killed the engine and unlocked the doors.

She needed to get away from Adam, needed to rethink this crazy scheme and make sure there wasn't another way to accomplish her goal.

Admit it. There is no other way. You've pursued every other avenue. This is your best chance to uncover the truth.

Clutching her purse and the file containing the prenuptial agreement and marriage contract, she sprang from the car before he could circle to her side. "You don't need to walk me to the door. The area is well-lit and safe."

He grasped her elbow in a warm, firm grip. Even though he'd touched her dozens of times tonight her breath still caught on contact. "Which way to the elevators?"

He obviously planned to ignore what she'd said.

"There are no elevators. I'm on the third floor."

He swept his free hand toward the stairwell.

Reluctantly, Lauryn led the way, but even with her "leading" he was right beside her, matching his steps to hers. She didn't want him in her apartment. Not that there was anything wrong with the tiny, tidy space, but after seeing the luxury to which he was accustomed, her place felt dinky and inadequate. The Art Deco building had been renovated, but with white-collar instead of wealthy tenants in mind.

She hiked the stairs with him by her side, unlocked the door and entered. A quick glance revealed she hadn't left anything lying around that she didn't want him to see—like the thick folder she'd compiled on her mother. Or the thinner one on Adam and his business clearly marked with his name on the tab.

She faced him with the marriage file clutched to her chest. "I'm in. Safe and sound. Thanks for taking me to the Ainsleys' tonight and for showing me your house."

He stepped forward, forcing her to shuffle hastily out of the way. With his eyes sweeping her space, the tiny kitchenette to the left, the sitting room in front of him, the doors leading to the small bedroom and minuscule bathroom, he shrugged off his suit jacket and hung it over the back of a kitchen chair.

"What are you doing?"

"Making myself comfortable."

"You don't have to stay. I'll look these over and bring them to work with me in the morning." She remained by the open door, hoping he'd take the hint, get his coat and leave.

Instead, he unbuttoned his cuffs and rolled up one shirtsleeve and then the other, revealing hair-dusted forearms. "I'll go over the documents with you."

"No need. If I have questions I'll write them down."

He prowled toward her, his blue gaze intent and unwavering, and palmed the door shut. "Trying to get rid of me, Lauryn?"

Her mouth dried and her pulse kicked erratically. "I have to get up early."

"It's only eleven and your boss will cut you some slack."

"I can't be late. I have to issue a check to the liquor supplier when he delivers first thing tomorrow."

"The truck comes at ten. You can sleep in. We have a few more details to work out." He parked his hands on his hips as if expecting an argument.

"Like what?"

"Like how you'll be paid. Brandon has spelled it out in

the marriage contract, but I'll recap. You'll receive just over forty-one grand every month. The first payment will be transferred into your account after the wedding ceremony."

"Why monthly?"

"So you won't skip out before the end of the second year."

"Once I give my word I don't break it." Not anymore. "But okay. Monthly is fine." She wasn't in this for the money anyway.

"I'll open bank and charge accounts for you. Because of the temporary nature of this marriage our money will be kept separate. If you blow your salary before the end of the month you're out of luck. I won't give you a dime more." When she didn't argue he continued, "And I'm going to hire an assistant for you."

"Wait a minute. You said I could keep my job, and I've told you, I don't need an assistant."

"I'll allow you to continue working, but only part-time. If we're inseparable newlyweds you'll be expected to make regular appearances by my side at the club. That means late nights. Your assistant will cover mornings."

His logic made sense. She reluctantly conceded by inclining her head. "What else?"

"A certain amount of PDAs will be required to make this marriage look real." He stood almost a yard away, but the distance and her apartment suddenly seemed to shrink.

"PDAs?"

"Public displays of affection. We'll need to touch. Like we did tonight."

She could handle that. "Okay."

"Kiss."

She gulped. "I don't think—"

"Newlyweds kiss and touch. Often. Making people believe we can't keep our hands off each other is part of the performance."

Her lips seemed to throb beneath his gaze. Tension stretched between them. Would he kiss her tonight? To seal the deal? To test her acting ability? Her heart pounded so hard she felt light-headed.

"Can you handle that?"

"I…um…yes. I can handle kissing you." She hoped.

Adam turned abruptly and strolled deeper into the living room. Her lungs emptied in a rush.

"You need different clothes, makeup, hair, a manicure—"

"You want me to get a makeover?" She didn't know whether to be insulted or pleased. She'd been downplaying her looks for so long it had become second nature. Apparently, she'd become good at looking drab.

He hitched his pants and sat on her sofa. Such a masculine man on flowered chintz just looked…wrong somehow. "To be believable as my wife you're going to need a little flash and a lot of style."

"To compete with your usual bimbos, you mean?"

"There will be no competition. I told you, Lauryn, I won't be unfaithful despite your ridiculous insistence on celibacy."

She marched across the room and stopped in front of him. "It's not ridiculous."

He stretched his arms along the back of the sofa and let his gaze coast from her face to her breasts, waist, legs and then back up again. Goose bumps sprouted in the wake of his examination.

"We'll see who can hold out the longest. And when you break, you come to me. No one else."

She wanted to smack that smug smile off his face. "I won't break."

"We'll see. I'll hire a personal shopper to help you choose appropriate clothing and make the beauty appointments."

"I'll choose my own clothes and make my own appointments."

"Lauryn—"

"And I won't dress like a tramp."

His eyes narrowed. "I don't date tramps."

"Didn't your last girlfriend recently make the news for flashing a pantiless crotch shot at the paparazzi?"

"She wasn't my girlfriend."

"The media says differently." She futilely tried to massage the headache squeezing the back of her skull beneath her knot of hair. "I can dress myself and do all the rest."

He sat forward, forearms braced on his knees. "Not from what I've seen. Keep your wardrobe conservative, but try to dress your age instead of matronly. Remember, people are supposed to believe I'm attracted to you."

Ouch. "You'll have to trust me."

"We can't afford mistakes. We have to get it right the first time."

"I'll get it right."

Tense, silent seconds ticked past. "You have a headache?"

"Yes. But it's nothing a good night's sleep won't cure. Please, Adam, go home. I'll read the documents and discuss them with you tomorrow."

He stared at her as if considering refusing, but then rose. "I'll pick you up at Estate at five tomorrow evening. We'll stop by Brandon's office for the notary to witness our signatures before going to dinner."

And then she'd be tied to Adam Garrison in a sham of a marriage for two years.

But what was two years when her entire life had been a lie?

Four

"Ready to roll?"

Lauryn nearly jumped out of her chair at the sound of Adam's voice behind her late Tuesday afternoon. She swiveled around and found him standing just inside her office.

Black suit, white shirt, conservative black-and-silver-patterned tie. Manly. Magnificent. He'd always been a sharp dresser, but she rarely saw him so formally attired.

"Almost. You're early. Let me print this last page." She caught the sheet before it could hit the tray. "I typed up an addendum."

"Addendum to what?" He crossed to her desk and took the papers she offered.

"Our agreement. These are the items we covered last night."

His gaze ricocheted from the pages to her face. He backtracked and closed her office door. "Our sex life is not going into a legal document."

"I want the terms spelled out."

"I won't have anything in writing that the press can use to discredit me. The prenup and marriage contract are risky enough. Delete that file," he ordered in an authoritative voice.

Her hackles rose in a conditioned response. Like a Pavlovian pooch. She'd never taken orders well. Her father had barked them as if she'd been a new recruit, and she…well, she'd rebelled. More often than not her response had landed her in hot water.

But that was then.

"Adam—"

"Do it now, Lauryn."

Grasping the arms of her chair, she sat back and counted to ten. "You're protecting your interests. Why shouldn't I protect mine?"

"I give you my word I will abide by your requests." He fed the pages into the shredder and then planted his palms on her desk and slowly leaned forward until he towered over her. He held her gaze without blinking. "Until you tell me otherwise."

The last phrase, delivered with a cocky half smile, oozed confidence and charisma. He thought she'd change her mind about the sex ban. He had no clue what kind of lockdown she'd put on her hormones since dissolving her hasty marriage or how good she'd become at ignoring the opposite sex. But he'd learn.

She deleted the file and even emptied her computer's recycle bin. "Done."

"Let's go."

"Wait. You need to approve the advertisement for my assistant."

"No need to advertise. Your predecessor is eager to come back to work. She's discovered she needs a break from full-time diaper duty."

Tension squeezed Lauryn's throat like an invisible strangler's hand. Silently, she collected her purse and the marriage agreement and followed Adam out of the building.

"Did your attorney look at the contract?" he asked.

"I don't have an attorney here and there wasn't time to find one."

Adam grasped her elbow and stopped her on the sidewalk. He met her gaze head-on. "I won't cheat you. The settlement is fair."

"I know. I read it." Five times. Pages of emotionless words promising twenty-four months of her life to a virtual stranger. A year to get Adam elected and then a year to keep him in office until he'd proven he could do the job.

Would she be able to remain as detached when she shared a home and a life with this man? Would she be able to walk away as if the marriage had never happened? Her reaction to Adam's stimulating touch said the time wouldn't pass without leaving its mark.

But she could control her body. Couldn't she?

She had to.

She turned, pulling free of his hand, and looked past him, but she didn't see his BMW by the curb. A dark blue Lexus sat in Adam's usual spot. It wasn't the first time someone had ignored the sign marking his reserved parking place. She scanned the street, but didn't see Adam's convertible in any of the other spaces, and the valet wouldn't arrive until later this evening. That meant a hike to the parking deck, which was one of the reasons—besides the prohibitive cost of parking—Lauryn always rode the bus. Thank goodness for her preference for flat-heeled shoes.

Adam reached into his pocket, withdrew a key ring and hit a button. The Lexus's lights flashed. He dangled the keys in front of her. "You wear a lot of blue. I hope that means you like it."

"What?" She gaped at the small SUV and then at him. "You're kidding, right?"

"No. You're driving." When she didn't reach for the keys he caught her hand, pressed them into her palm and closed her fingers around them.

She didn't know which startled her more. The pricey car or the contact with Adam. She'd have to work harder at reining in this taboo attraction. "I have a decent car."

"Now you have a better one. Keep the old one or sell it. I don't care."

"But…"

"Appearances, Lauryn. It's all about appearances." He checked traffic and then opened the driver's door for her. "Let's go. Brandon's staying after hours for us."

She slid into the buttery soft leather seat, filled her lungs with that new-car smell and checked out the tinted sunroof. Compared to her four-year-old economy sedan, this car's dashboard looked like something NASA built. GPS and satellite radio. Who knew what the other gizmos were? Her hand trembled as she slipped the key into the ignition and started the engine.

Adam climbed into the passenger seat. "You've delivered documents to Brandon for me before. Remember where his office is?"

"Yes." She wasn't looking forward to maneuvering a brand-new luxury vehicle through rush-hour traffic.

Adam gave her perhaps five minutes to get accustomed to the way the car handled before speaking again. "Bahamas law requires us to be in the country twenty-four hours before we can apply for a marriage license. We'll leave tomorrow morning, get married Thursday evening and then come home Monday morning and move our stuff into the house."

Thursday? She gulped. "So soon?"

"Waiting wastes time."

"You're willing to leave Estate that long?"

"The staff will survive without me, and Sandy will fill in for you."

He had it all figured out. "Sandy's my predecessor?"

"Yes."

"I won't have time for the makeover you requested by tomorrow."

She kept her eyes on traffic but caught his shrug out of the corner of her eye. "Do it on the island. Cassie's well put-together. She can tell you where to go."

All too soon they reached the high-rise housing Washington & Associates. Because so many of the building's workers were making the evening exodus, Lauryn easily found a spot near the entrance. She parked and climbed from the car. The knot between her shoulders from driving the unfamiliar vehicle sank to her stomach and expanded with each step she took beside Adam toward their destination.

He ushered her into the elevator and up to the law offices of Washington & Associates. A woman Lauryn guessed to be in her sixties waited for them by the reception desk with a big smile lined on her face. On past visits Lauryn had always left packages with the receptionist, who wasn't behind her desk.

"What is this I hear about an engagement? Both of your brothers, then Brandon and now you. Have the men in Miami suddenly become smarter?"

"Hello Rachel." Adam pulled the diminutive woman into a hug and then released her and extended his hand toward Lauryn. "This is Lauryn Lowes, my fiancée. Lauryn, this is Rachel Suarez."

Lauryn reluctantly put her left hand in Adam's and let him tug her forward. The shocking heat of his touch seeped up her arm and then oozed down deep inside her, but the woman thankfully broke the spell by enfolding Lauryn's right hand in both of hers.

"He'll be a good husband as long as you keep him on a short leash," she whispered.

Wide-eyed, Lauryn darted a quick glance at Adam to see if he'd heard, but his face remained impassive.

"Thanks for that tip," she replied and received a wink in return.

Movement down the hall drew Lauryn's attention. Brandon Washington strolled toward them. He was Adam's height, attractive and African-American. Lauryn had spoken with him on numerous occasions when he stopped by Estate.

The men shook hands and clapped shoulders before Brandon greeted her with a nod. Lauryn nodded back and tried to smile.

Adam indicated Mrs. Suarez. "Is she still running this place?"

"She likes to think so," Brandon replied. The warmth in his eyes belied his firm voice. "Let's step into my office." Brandon turned to Mrs. Suarez. "Give us five minutes and then join us, please."

Lauryn's mouth dried. The deal was all but done. Her feet felt weighted as she followed the men across the carpet. The point of no return lay directly ahead.

But if she walked away what would she have learned about her mother? Not enough. Not nearly enough. And she'd probably lose her job, too, for leading Adam on and then reneging.

The door closed behind them, sealing them into Brandon's office. He faced them across his desk and waited until they were seated before asking Adam, "Are you sure you want to do this?"

"I'm sure."

Dark brown eyes lasered in on Lauryn's. "Are you?"

"I—" She covered her flash of panic by clearing her throat and handing over the folder. "I am."

Brandon accepted it and withdrew the prenuptial agreement and marriage contract. "Did you have any questions, Lauryn? Is there anything that requires clarification?"

Is there another way? "No."

"She didn't have a lawyer read the agreements," Adam said.

Brandon stilled. "Would you like me to have one of my associates come in and go over the documents? I can assure you he'd be unbiased."

"No. I'm comfortable with the contracts."

Brandon nodded. "Once you get to the Bahamas you'll have to provide proof of arrival time in the country. The airport should be able to give you that. Then you'll swear before the U.S. Consul at the American Embassy that you're single American citizens who wish to get married. The next day you'll visit the Registrar General's office to get your license. No blood tests are required, but Adam says you're both going to be tested tomorrow morning anyway. Good decision."

That was news. Lauryn looked at Adam. He stared back. He must really believe he'd be able to charm her into bed.

Not going to happen, she told him silently with her eyes.

One corner of his mouth lifted, and she could practically hear his thoughts. *Wanna bet?*

"Lauryn, are you divorced or widowed?" Brandon asked as he laid the documents on the desk in front of them.

"Um…no." She'd been told annulments didn't count. Legally it was as if her marriage had never happened, which was only fitting since she couldn't remember the ceremony. Her skin burned with shame over that low point in her life. She'd just as soon nobody ever knew how stupid she'd been.

"Then that's all the paperwork you'll need. Cassie has arranged the rental of a cottage for you on a private beach. She's also hired the minister, photographer and caterers. The ceremony will take place Thursday evening on the beach at sunset. Cassie and I will be your witnesses. I'll issue a press release afterward. Any questions?".

Cold permeated Lauryn's hands and feet. She shook her head because she couldn't have spoken even if she'd tried.

A tap sounded on the door. It opened and Mrs. Suarez poked her salt-and-pepper head through the gap. "Ready for me?"

"Perfect timing as always," Brandon answered.

The petite woman bustled in carrying her notary stamp.

Brandon offered Lauryn a pen. "Lauryn, you sign first."

It took a second to find her nerve. She accepted the pen with an almost steady hand and scratched her name and the date where he indicated, first on the marriage contract and then on the prenuptial agreement. Adam did the same. And then Mrs. Suarez affixed her notary stamp, date and signature to each.

Done.

Heavy doubts rumbled through Lauryn like a California mud slide followed by a weird kind of numbness as Brandon matter-of-factly collected the documents and returned them to the file folder.

"I'll make sure you each have copies and I'll see you Thursday." Brandon stood and then extended his hand.

Thursday.

In forty-eight hours she'd be a married woman. Again.

And this time she couldn't call daddy to fix her mistake.

* * *

"Will you marry me, Lauryn?"

Stunned, Lauryn stared at Adam. The buzz in her ears drowned out the conversations around them in the elegant, exclusive restaurant. Or maybe a hush had fallen over the eavesdropping patrons awaiting her response.

She didn't know much about diamonds, but she'd bet the one pinched between Adam's finger and thumb cost a mint. The marquis stone had to be at least two carats. She forced her gaze from the mesmerizing sparkler to his eyes. Serious. Compelling. Intensely blue.

"I—I—"

Even though they hadn't rehearsed this, even though he'd surprised her with this very public proposal, she knew what she was supposed to say. She just couldn't get her mouth to work.

Flowers. Crystal. Candlelight. A strolling violinist. A prime table overlooking the bay. Adam had planned the perfect setting for a proposal.

And it was all fake. As fake as their marriage would be.

"Lauryn, baby, don't leave me hanging. You know we belong together."

She heard the warning in his deep voice and pressed a hand over her frantically beating heart. This wasn't right. And yet what choice did she have if she wanted to learn the truth?

Answer the man.

"Y-yes," she heard herself say. "Yes, Adam, I'll marry you."

A spattering of applause startled and embarrassed her. These days she hated being a spectacle as much as she'd once thrived on such attention. She briefly squeezed her eyes shut and then met Adam's gaze. He wore a wide smile—one that didn't reach his eyes—as he slipped the ring on her finger. And then he stood and pulled her into his arms.

His mouth covered hers so quickly she froze in shock. She hadn't expected such a public first kiss, nor had she expected his mouth to be soft. Or gentle. Or warm. Or persuasive. Or delicious. He sipped from her lips the way he had from his wineglass earlier.

Not that she'd been watching his mouth. Much.

He lifted his head a fraction of an inch, leaning his forehead against hers. "Put your arms around my neck."

His lips brushed hers with each whispered word and the eroticism nearly melted her. She lifted her arms as directed and his hands tightened on her waist, pulling her closer. The embrace mashed her breasts against the hard, hot wall of his chest and fused her hips to his. Desire swept through her like a California canyon fire, searing her deep inside. She planted her hands against his lapels, broke the kiss and looked away—right into the eyes of Helene Ainsley two tables away.

It's all about appearances, Adam had said.

And Lauryn had better not forget it. That's all this was. A charade. A setup. A chance for him to paint a convincing picture for the business council nominating committee. The heat in Lauryn's veins turned to ice.

Adam reclaimed her hand and carried it to his lips. He kissed her knuckle below the ring and reseated her. Leaning over her, he caressed her shoulders and then pressed another scorching kiss to the tender skin beneath her ear. Goose bumps rose on her skin.

Not good. She really, *really* didn't want to want him.

"Very convincing. Good job," he murmured low enough that only she could hear.

The waiter arrived immediately with a bottle of champagne and presented the label for inspection.

Oh yes, Adam had definitely planned this—right down to preordering his favorite vintage of the Salon Blanc champagne. Lauryn knew his preferences because the club kept the brand in stock. Rumor had it that when he requested a bottle he'd chosen his bedmate for the night.

Lauryn didn't want to be just another woman to share his sheets and his champagne. She'd better not forget the Adam Garrisons of this world bought what they wanted.

He might have bought her participation, but he couldn't buy her self-respect. And that meant she had to stay out of his bed no matter how easily he'd awoken the passionate hedonist she thought she'd buried years ago. Because when the hedonist came out to play, her common sense went away.

And she refused to be another man's puppet.

Lauryn stopped dead on the asphalt. "What is that?"

"A Columbia 400, turbo," Adam said with enough pride in his voice to clamp an iron band around Lauryn's chest. "My plane. Your ride," he added, confirming her worst fears.

He covered the last ten yards in quick, long strides and set their luggage down beside a tiny white airplane with a shiny propeller on its nose. His hand dipped into his pocket, reappearing with a set of keys.

She closed her eyes and gulped. This is so not good.

She should have known he wasn't just taking a different route to Miami International when he headed west of town.

Lauryn's shaking legs carried her forward at a much slower pace. "Why can't we fly commercial? You know, big jets with trained pilots, copilots and air hostesses who bring drinks?"

"Too slow." He shoved his aviator sunglasses into his hair and looked directly into her eyes as if he believed his calm assuredness would be contagious. "I am a trained pilot. I've had a license since I turned sixteen. You'll be safe with me."

Someone called out to him. Adam turned and walked to meet a guy in a khaki flight suit coming out of one of the hangars.

"I do not have a death wish," she muttered.

"Neither do I," he called over his shoulder.

She waited until he finished his conversation and returned. "I've never flown in a private plane."

"Good. I'll be your first, and I'll make it good for you." The gleam in his eyes as he opened a door on the side of the aircraft was purely sexual. Her body responded accordingly, warming, moistening. She shook off the unwanted response.

"My father died in a plane crash."

Compassion softened Adam's features. "I'm sorry. I didn't know. I take good care of my plane and I'll take care of you."

She wavered.

"Statistically, you're less likely to be in an accident in a plane than in a car. Climb in. Sit in the right front seat."

Her feet stayed planted. "Adam, I get seasick."

"Seasick and airsick are not the same. Trust me, Lauryn."

He grabbed her cold hands and carried them to the warmth of his cheeks, sandwiching her icy fingers between his smooth-shaven jaw and his warm palms. And then he leaned in and kissed her. One gentle, coaxing caress of his lips against hers followed another and another until the beginnings of arousal edged the fear from her stiff limbs. She was on the verge of responding, of threading her fingers through his hair and pulling him closer, when he lifted his head.

"Trust me," he repeated.

She was stuck. He was going to force her to ride in that dinky tin can. Grimacing, she pulled her hands free. "On three conditions. A, if I absolutely hate it you let me fly home on a regular plane. B, no fancy acrobatics. And C, I don't want to hear anything about the mile-high club. Not one word."

He grinned. "Deal. Now climb in."

He handed her into a compartment barely four feet high and wide. There were two leather bucket seats in the cabin and two more up front. She squeezed between the front seats and groaned as she sank into the one on the right. She was surrounded by glass, and she'd be able to see exactly how high they were off the ground. She buckled her seat belt. Tight.

She couldn't believe her father had flown for a living. Flying hadn't just been his job, it had been his passion.

Ten minutes later Adam eased his long frame in beside her. She gripped the armrests and watched him prepare for flight. Headset. Buttons. Dozens of them. And the she noticed the twin screens on the dash. One was GPS. She couldn't identify the other one. The propeller started, vibrating the plane.

He leaned over and pushed a headset over her hair. "Can you hear me now?"

He winked. Her stomach knotted. She closed her eyes.

Minutes passed while Adam communicated with the tower in the take-charge voice he used at work. She occupied herself with mental math. How much interest would a million dollars paid in twenty-four installments net over five years, ten, by retirement age?

The plane moved forward, bouncing gently down the runway before gathering speed and lifting off. She knew the exact second they left the ground. Squeezing her eyes closed, she tightened her grip on the armrests.

Moments later Adam's hand covered hers. "You can look now."

She eased open one eye and saw blue sky. She opened the other and risked looking down. Her stomach contents didn't rush to her throat. If anything, she wanted to see more and leaned closer to the window to do so. She could even identify some of the landmarks.

"The water's so green."

"Beautiful, isn't it? Same color as your eyes."

She snapped her head toward him and met his gaze. *Forget it. He's a natural-born charmer. Compliments come as easily to him as breathing.* But knowing the truth didn't lessen the impact of his words. "Thank you."

"Want to fly over the club and the estate before we head east?"

She considered it, realized she didn't feel the least bit sick and nodded. "Yes. I'd like that."

He didn't have to be nice. He had her where he wanted her, had her contracted to do exactly as he wished.

But it touched her that he made an effort.

Like a deer trapped in the headlights, Adam couldn't turn away from the view outside the window.

Mouthwatering curves. Amazing legs.

Cassie said something to Lauryn as the women walked toward the trunk of Cassie's car and Lauryn looked up at the cottage. Her gaze collided with his and the air dammed in his lungs.

She's beautiful. How had he missed that?

The raw material had to have been there because there was no way Lauryn could have worked major miracles in the five hours since Cassie had met their plane at the Nassau airport and whisked Lauryn away for an afternoon of shopping and…whatever. Adam had been more than happy to dodge that bullet by picking up the car Garrison, Inc. kept on the island and driving it and their luggage to the house.

Cassie hauled a number of shopping bags from the trunk and passed them to Lauryn. Adam snapped out of his trance and headed for the door. His legs felt rubbery as he jogged down the stairs. He blamed it on the blood drawn at his doctor's this morning and knew he lied.

He stopped beside the women. Adrenaline pulsed through his veins making him hyperaware of his bride-to-be. Sunlight gleamed off the hair streaming over Lauryn's shoulders. He'd never seen her hair down, and the urge to test the texture of the champagne-gold strands nearly overwhelmed him.

Thick lashes surrounded her sea-green eyes and a shell-pink gloss coated her lips. The breeze carried her incredible scent.

"Hello again, Adam."

He heard the smile in Cassie's voice and forced his stunned gaze from Lauryn to his grinning half sister. She seemed to be enjoying his stupefaction. "Thanks for helping, Cassie."

"My pleasure. So what do you think?"

His gaze devoured Lauryn from her satiny hair to her pink-painted toenails. He couldn't begin to put his thoughts into words. How had he ever believed her plain? Had he been so self-absorbed he'd missed the prize right in front of his face?

Apparently so.

"This cottage is one of my favorites," Cassie continued.

He jerked his attention back to his half sister. She meant the beach house? "It's very nice. Comfortable. Private."

"Excellent. I have to run. I have a hot date tonight with your best man. See you tomorrow."

"Bye, Cassie, and thanks again," Lauryn called out as Cassie climbed in her car.

"You're welcome. I had fun."

Adam watched the car pull away and then took another long look at Lauryn. He cursed the months of celibacy since his father's death. Despite what the tabloids said, Adam hadn't been in the mood to let anyone get close lately—not even physically. As peeved as he was with his father for refusing to acknowledge his accomplishments even after death, Adam still missed the old man.

Bags rattled as Lauryn shifted in her high-heeled sandals—sandals that made her legs look endless.

"Let me have those." He relieved her of her load, carried the loot inside to the room he'd chosen for her and dumped the bags on her bed. There were fewer bags than he'd expected. He'd expected her to try to bankrupt him.

Lauryn entered behind him. She scanned the space and then crossed the tile floor to peek into the luxurious bathroom. Her heels added a hypnotizing sway to her hips that he hadn't noticed before.

Her conservative clothing didn't scream "do me" like so many of Estate's patrons did. But there was a subtle sexiness in the way her new sundress skimmed her curves that yanked his awakened libido like an angler setting his hook.

Last night's kiss at the restaurant had rocked him with a tsunami of unexpected hunger. The one at the airport this morning had rocked him, too. And that was before he'd seen his soon-to-be wife looking like this.

He wanted her. Need pulsed in his gut. But he'd promised to abide by her no-sex rule until she said otherwise.

And dammit, he prided himself on being a man of his word.

That didn't mean he wouldn't try to change her mind. But

not until after the wedding. Judging by the wariness in her eyes if he tried to seduce her tonight he'd be missing a fiancée before the ceremony tomorrow.

"My bedroom's across the den." Desire roughened his voice.

"Okay." She looked and sounded relieved.

If he wanted to sleep better tonight than he had last night he needed to get out of this room, out of this house before he started picturing Lauryn wearing nothing but sleek, wet skin and a dusting of bubbles in that whirlpool tub. With him beside or beneath her.

Too late. He stifled a groan.

"Where are your glasses?" he asked in an attempt to sideline his illicit thoughts.

White teeth pinched her bottom lip and she wrinkled her nose. She looked so damned adorably guilty he almost whimpered. "I…um, don't really need them."

"Why in the hell did you hide behind shapeless clothing and ugly glasses?" It made no sense. The women he knew flaunted their assets. Hell, they paid good money to have bigger, better assets implanted.

"I learned not to draw attention to my looks a long time ago. Men assume if you're pretty, you're stupid and available."

"And you aren't available?" He knew she wasn't stupid.

"Not at the moment."

Her flip response stirred something unfamiliar in him. Possessiveness? No. *Determination* to make sure this plan worked. He couldn't afford slip-ups if he wanted the council and his brothers to believe he'd fallen for his straightlaced accountant and settled down. "And you won't be until after we're divorced."

"That won't be a problem."

The certainty in her tone raised red flags. Holy hell, was she gay? Did that explain why no one had seen her on a date? South Beach had a large gay population. Was that the real reason she'd moved to Florida? Because her story about her father had seemed a lame reason to move three thousand miles.

No, Lauryn couldn't be gay. He hadn't imagined the attraction between them or the hunger in her eyes. He'd felt the softening of her lips beneath his when he'd kissed her, and he'd heard her breath catch each time he'd touched her.

He wanted to kiss her now. To prove his theory.

But he wouldn't. Not yet.

Even though his neglected hormones had him in a tailspin.

Forget the candles, flowers and prepared meals he'd asked Cassie to arrange so he and Lauryn could play out the love-birds-needing-privacy farce. He couldn't handle a romantic dinner on the deck tonight. He needed crowds. Loud music. A noisy restaurant. Distractions. Anything but an intimate dinner for two.

"We're eating out tonight. Be ready in ten."

Lauryn's brow creased. "Cassie said she'd filled the refrigerator with local dishes for us."

Damn. He'd hoped his half sister had neglected to mention that detail. "She did."

Lauryn swept back her champagne locks with a newly manicured hand tipped in pearl-pink polish. The muscles of Adam's abdomen ripped as if she'd scraped those short nails across his flesh.

"Adam, I'd rather postpone the whole putting-on-a-show-for-the-locals thing, if you don't mind. I know we have to eventually, but it's our first night here and I'm kind of whipped. Cassie is a shopping machine. Surely if anyone is paying attention to our itinerary they'd expect us to want to be alone sometimes?"

Now that she mentioned it, he could see her fatigue in the faint shadows beneath her eyes and the slight downward turn of her mouth.

For sanity's sake he should be a bastard and insist on going out, but instead he ground his teeth on a frustrated curse.

It was going to be a long night.

"Pick whatever you want to eat and shove it in the microwave. I'm going for a run. I'll be back in an hour."

And then Adam did something he'd never done before.

He ran from a woman.

Five

Thursday. Her wedding day.

Lauryn had never been claustrophobic before, but she was getting there fast. The walls of the spacious oceanfront bedroom seemed to close in around her as the clock inched toward the time set for the ceremony. Her pulse raced and her mouth felt as dry and gritty as the sand dunes outside the cottage.

The silk chiffon of her strapless ivory tea-length dress fluttered against her shins as she paced from the window to the door and back, again and again, and the lace bolero jacket abraded her neck and shoulders. Since the ceremony would take place on the beach she'd decided against wearing shoes, and the floor tiles further chilled her already cold bare feet.

Cold feet. Appropriate.

She couldn't help comparing this wedding to her first. Her ex had had an agenda. So did Adam. Only Adam's wasn't illegal and no one would get hurt. Or arrested. Plus Lauryn knew what she was getting into this time. At least she hoped she did.

At eighteen and a day, she'd been incredibly young, naive and hardheaded when her father had forbidden her to see Tommy Saunders again. She'd foolishly believed herself old enough and wise enough to know better than her father. She and her dad had had another one of their legendary screaming matches, but this time Lauryn's mother hadn't played mediator the way she usually did when Lauryn's father went all dictatorial.

Afterward Lauryn had hidden in her room and called Tommy to vent. He'd insisted she was of age and her father couldn't tell her what to do anymore. On a wave of righteous indignation she'd agreed to go to Mexico with Tommy for spring break. Two days later she'd packed her bags, lied about spending the week at the beach with a girlfriend and left. Not one of her finest decisions.

In Tijuana Tommy had plied her with tequila and then asked her to marry him. She'd almost agreed, but even tipsy she'd known better than to cross her father that drastically.

The next morning she'd awoken hungover and with a cheap wedding ring on her finger that she couldn't remember putting there. When she'd freaked out Tommy had admitted he'd slipped something into her drink to loosen her inhibitions and help her make the decision he knew she really wanted to make.

His high-handedness had worried her but she'd loved him enough to make excuses for him. She hadn't panicked until he revealed his scheme over lunch to make them both rich and then she'd suddenly felt queasy and afraid.

Blaming her hangover, she'd excused herself to go to the bathroom, slipped out the backdoor of the cantina, found a phone and called her father.

That was the last time Lauryn had rebelled. After her father had rescued her from that disaster she'd become the perfect dutiful daughter, a straight-A student and as prim and proper as Emily Post.

Emily Post wouldn't be eloping in the Bahamas or neglecting to invite her mother to the ceremony.

Wincing, Lauryn paused by the glass doors leading to the deck. She hadn't called because she didn't want her mother to know about this marriage. Susan would be upset at how far Lauryn was willing to go to gain information about her birthmother, and she'd be hurt. She'd view this as another sign that she'd failed Lauryn as a parent. But other than not revealing the secret of Lauryn's birthmother sooner, that couldn't be further from the truth.

Lauryn studied the beach below her bedroom and tried to calm her agitated nerves. The flowered archway Cassie had ordered for the ceremony stood in the sand between the cottage and the lapping waves. The photographer hustled around checking shot angles or light or whatever it was photographers did.

The doorbell followed by muffled voices penetrated the closed bedroom door. Was that Cassie? The need to see a friendly face overwhelmed her. Lauryn yanked open the door.

Adam, Brandon and Cassie turned in unison.

"I take it you're not superstitious," Cassie said.

"I'm not." Lauryn's gaze slid to Adam as if dragged by a strong riptide. A black tuxedo complimented his ink-dark hair, made his shoulders look broader and his legs longer. His white shirt accentuated his tan and made his blue eyes and the flash of teeth in his slow smile seem brighter. He looked like every girl's fantasy groom. Handsome. Wealthy.

Sexy.

She tamped down that thought and dampened her dry lips.

No one will respect or value you if you don't respect and value yourself, her father's words came back to her.

So no sex and no more Mr. Right Nows. Not even the one she'd marry in a few minutes.

"If it's bad luck for the bride and groom to see each other before the ceremony then we're already cursed. Adam and I spent most of the day driving from one official's office to another's dealing with the legalities of this…marriage."

Adam crossed the room, looped his arms around her waist and pulled her close. Lauryn stiffened automatically. She couldn't let him keep getting to her like he'd done at the restaurant and airport. The heat of his body singed her at every contact point—breasts, waist, hips, thighs. He feathered his lips across hers and then lifted his head a fraction of an inch. Warning flashed in his eyes.

"You look beautiful, Lauryn."

Even knowing his compliment was part of the act didn't stifle the pleasure his words sent eddying through her.

"Thank you. So do you." Her cheeks warmed. She briefly ducked her head before daring to look into his eyes again. "I mean, you look good in a tux."

He dipped his head again. She forced herself to remain passive as he sipped from her lips once, twice more. Her heart raced and desire tugged like an undercurrent in her belly. She'd have to get used to being handled by him, kissed by him. But she had to shut down her response.

She heard Cassie's sigh. The woman believed this to be a true love match. Lauryn liked her new friend too much to lie to her, but Adam had ordered her to keep their secret.

Ordered. The back of Lauryn's neck prickled.

Only Brandon knew the truth behind this hasty marriage and Adam wanted to keep it that way.

On the pretext of examining the small wedding cake

sitting in the center of the dining room table Lauryn wiggled free. Adam let her go, but she could feel his gaze on her back. She fought the urge to lick her lips and lost. His taste lingered on her mouth and left her hungry for more.

Two bottles of champagne waited in sterling silver ice buckets on a sideboard and through the open kitchen door she spotted a pair of workers hustling around preparing food, presumably for the feast after the ceremony. Brandon, Cassie and the minister were staying for a wedding dinner. As much as Lauryn dreaded the lovey-dovey pretense, having company meant delaying the time alone with her groom, and that was good.

Last night… She exhaled slowly, trying to ease her over-stretched nerves. Last night had been a nightmare. She couldn't remember ever being so aware of another person. Every shift of Adam's body on the sofa, each rustle of his clothing or chink of his glass on the coffee table had sounded as loud as a ship's horn. Finally, tension had driven Lauryn to her room for an early night of reading. *Attempted reading.* But a romance with steamy love scenes wasn't what she needed when she wanted to douse any potential flames for her groom. Even with the door closed she'd been aware of Adam's movements throughout the cottage.

Their marriage might be a business deal, but the whole wedding thing seemed so real. So…permanent. But it wasn't. And she didn't want it to be. One day she'd find the right man to build a future with—one who'd marry her because he loved her and not because he had a hidden agenda for marrying.

Like her father had had for marrying Susan. Like Tommy and Adam had for marrying Lauryn. Surely all men weren't that conniving? There had to be some good guys out there somewhere, and when this was over she'd find one.

She forced a smile and turned back to the trio in the den. "Cassie, this is incredible. I can't believe you pulled it all together so quickly."

"I've enjoyed it. Besides, it's good practice for when Brandon and I get married."

"And when is that going to be?" Adam asked.

"Soon," Brandon replied firmly with his dark eyes intent on Cassie.

Lauryn wanted a man who looked at her the way Brandon looked at Cassie—with his love shining like a lighthouse beacon from his eyes.

A brisk knock at the front door made Lauryn jump. Adam headed into the foyer and returned moments later with a dark-skinned, black-suited, white-collared minister by his side. Adam made the introductions.

Lauryn barely heard him through the alarms shrieking like hungry seagulls in her head. She wanted to run. All the way back to California. But she couldn't. Not until she found her answers.

She dug her toes into the rough sisal rug and the movement drew Adam's attention.

"Excuse me," he said and left the room. Moments later he returned without his shoes and socks. Lauryn's heart blipped irregularly. Adam had looked sexy before, but there was something dangerously appealing about a barefooted, tux-clad man that made her insides feel like a lava lamp.

His eyes met Lauryn's. "The sun is on the horizon. Ready?"

No. "Yes."

"Shall we?" He crooked his elbow in invitation.

Under a deluge of doubts Lauryn hesitated for precious seconds and then hooked her arm through Adam's. His muscles shifted beneath her fingers and her nerves and legs quivered.

He handed her a single long-stemmed red rose with an ivory ribbon twined around the thornless stem and then led her out the back door, down the porch stairs and across the warm sand to the archway.

An ocean breeze teased her hair, lifting the unbound strands and pulling at the wreath of flowers she wore instead of a veil. Adam caught a stray lock and smoothed it behind her ear. His fingertips glided down the hollow of her neck. She shivered. With awareness. With lust. Neither of which were welcome.

Cassie and Brandon flanked them and the beaming minister took his place and launched into the vows. At any other time Lauryn would have found the man's melodious accented voice beautiful, but the fragrant frame of the arch seemed to enclose her as securely as a locked jail cell.

A cold fog descended over her. She couldn't believe she was marrying a man she didn't love to find out more about a woman who'd discarded her.

But why hadn't Adrianna wanted her? That question kept Lauryn from running. She had to know. And she was counting on Adam's house holding the answers.

Adam's warm hands tightened around Lauryn's icy fingers. Did he sense her doubts? Her growing panic?

Too late to back out now.

As if he were willing her to finish what they'd started, his gaze never left hers as he stated his vows in a deep, steady baritone. If he had any doubts about the deception they were perpetrating he concealed them well. His hands were steady as he slid a platinum diamond eternity band onto her trembling finger next to the sparkling marquis.

And then it was Lauryn's turn. She numbly repeated the words the minister fed her and prayed this wasn't as big a mistake as her first wedding. She'd trusted Tommy and he'd betrayed her. Would Adam do the same?

She looked at the strong hand in her palm as she eased the wide platinum band they'd bought this morning over Adam's knuckle. Because he'd refused to put their amended agreement in writing, only his word would keep him from consummating their marriage tonight. Or any other night. Could she trust him?

A little late to worry about that now, isn't it?

A whirlpool of mixed emotions churned within her. This was so wrong. She was taking vows. Vows she had no intention of keeping. And yet what other choice did she have?

"I now pronounce you *mon*," the minister pronounced island-style, "and wife. Congratulations Mr. and Mrs. Garrison."

Mrs. Garrison.

Before she could digest those words Adam cupped her face in his palms and covered her mouth with his. This wasn't a tentative seal-the-deal peck. Adam kissed like a man assured of his welcome. His mouth branded hers, stamping her with ownership, and then his tongue separated her lips and swept the sensitive inside of her mouth as if he had every right to be there.

Tasting. Teasing. Tempting.

His kiss invited her to a party of sensual delights she had no doubt a man of his experience could provide. She hadn't had a lover since Tommy, and he'd been a twenty-three-year-old selfish jerk. The men before Tommy had been just as clumsy, just as selfish.

Adam's kiss promised satisfaction and she felt her control slipping. He overwhelmed her senses with his taste, his scent, his touch, and her hormones did a rain dance in hopes of ending the nine-year drought. The kiss felt so good, so right, that she lost herself in a hot rush of need, dug her toes in the shifting sand and pushed herself deeper into his embrace. Every inch of her body yearned to accept his invitation, to find out if lovemaking could actually be as good as it was in the romance novels she read.

She vaguely registered the birds screeching overhead, the waves crashing nearby, but it was Cassie's laughter that jarred Lauryn back to reality.

What are you doing?

She ripped her mouth free.

Adam breathed harshly. Hunger blazed in his eyes as he held her gaze, and she realized her mistake. She'd done a lot of less than honorable things in her time, things that made her cringe with shame. But she'd never been a tease.

That kiss, laden with years of pent-up passion, had promised something she had no intention of delivering.

"Sober enough to come to the phone?"

Lauryn nearly choked on her champagne when she heard Adam's question as she reentered the den after changing out of her wedding dress.

Okay, so maybe this was her second glass since Cassie and Brandon had left, and she'd had one two hours ago after dinner with her slice of wedding cake. Still, she should switch to coffee unless she wanted another wedding night like her first. One she couldn't remember. Drowning her nerves and her doubts wasn't working, anyway.

Adam's discarded tux jacket draped the back of a nearby chair. He stood facing the darkness outside the glass doors with both elbows bent beside his head and his white dress shirt stretched taut across his broad shoulders. The table lamp reflected off his wedding band drawing her attention to the cell phone pressed to his left ear.

"I'll wait while you get her, Lisette."

Lauryn realized he wasn't talking to her.

He turned. His gaze collided with hers and then slowly

drifted over her navy knit polo top, past her khaki knee-length shorts to her legs, bare feet and back up again. He'd unfastened his tie and the top three buttons of his shirt, but he looked tense instead of relaxed.

Welcome to the club.

He angled the phone away from his mouth. "I'm calling my mother to tell her about the wedding. Need to call anyone?"

Guilt sank its teeth into her like a great white shark. "No. Thanks."

"Do you have any family? I didn't ask or give you the option of having someone at the ceremony."

"There's only my…mother. But she's leaving in a few days for a fifteen-day South Pacific cruise. I didn't want to bother her."

Susan and Lauryn's father had booked the cruise before he died. Rather than cancel the trip Susan had decided to go in his memory and had asked Lauryn to accompany her. But Lauryn wasn't ready yet. Not ready to forgive the lie or to give up on her quest to learn about her birthmother.

"You're not concerned she'll hear about our marriage from another source? Brandon's sending out a press release tomorrow."

"She lives in Sacramento. I can't see the newspapers out there carrying the story. Can you?"

"Probably not."

"I'll tell her when she gets back." Or never. Lauryn had already disappointed Susan in a dozen different ways. Why do so again, especially now when their relationship was already strained?

His gaze raked her again. She bit her lip. Ever since that blasted wedding kiss he'd looked at her differently. Sexually. As if she'd slipped into something from Frederick's of Hollywood instead of Lands' End.

That wasn't good.

He stiffened and turned back to the window. "Hello, Mother... I'm in the Bahamas. I called to tell you I got married this afternoon...to Lauryn Lowes, Estate's accountant.... No, you've never met her...."

Lauryn cringed. Rather than eavesdrop she retreated to the kitchen to give Adam privacy. She poured out the rest of her champagne, washed the flute and then put on the tea kettle more for something to do than for the need for caffeine. Her conscience probably wouldn't let her sleep tonight, anyway.

What would Adam's family think of this hasty wedding? Of her? She wasn't one of their affluent circle. At least, she hadn't been able to prove her connection yet. Would she ever? And would being Adrianna Laurence's illegitimate child be a detriment or an asset?

A sound made her turn. Adam stood on the threshold. "We need to make arrangements to move the stuff from your apartment into storage."

A mental door slammed shut. An escape route sealed. "My lease doesn't expire for months."

"You can sublet. For appearances' sake you need to vacate."

"I'll...I'll check into subletting." She knew wasting money on rent wasn't wise, but giving up her apartment seemed so...final.

She turned back to the mahogany variety box of Island Rose Tea, a Bahamian specialty, and dithered over her selection. Maybe the Cat Island Chamomile would calm her.

Fat chance.

Ever conscious of Adam watching and waiting only a few yards away, she found a mug in the cabinet and sugar on the counter and then pulled the creamer from the refrigerator.

When she could stall no longer she faced him. He'd propped a shoulder against the doorjamb. His hair looked a little more disheveled than usual, making her fingers itch to smooth it.

Ridiculous. No touching except when required by an audience.

"What did you tell your mother?" she asked. "About us, I mean. When Cassie asked today I didn't know what to say. We need to be to be on the same page."

"Agreed." His unwavering gaze made her fidgety. "What did you tell Cassie?"

She'd been caught off guard because she and Adam hadn't concocted a cover story. Reluctantly, Lauryn had admitted she'd developed a crush on Adam after meeting him at the initial interview. But she wasn't telling *him* that. "That we met at work and tried to keep our involvement quiet because fraternization is against Estate policy."

"That's good. I'll use that."

"But what did you tell your mother?"

"Just what you overheard. That I married Estate's accountant today. Mother wasn't sober enough to process more. You'll soon discover she has a drinking problem. If you want to have a coherent conversation with her then you have to do it before noon."

She heard suppressed anger—or was it frustration?—and maybe a hint of concern in his voice. "What about your brothers and sisters? Besides Cassie, you have two of each, right?"

"Right. My brothers, Parker and Stephen, are older, my sisters, Brooke and Brittany, the twins, are younger. I'll e-mail them."

"I don't have any siblings, but I can't imagine delivering such big news via an impersonal e-mail. Don't you want to call them?"

"We're not that close."

Sympathy welled within her—sympathy she couldn't afford
to feel for him if she wanted to keep her distance. At least he
had a family. Maybe it wasn't a perfect one, but he had them,
and if he wasn't close to them that was his fault. "But—"

The tea kettle shrieked, making her nearly jump out of her
skin.

Adam pushed off the jamb, turned off the stove and
removed the kettle from the burner. "Lauryn, it would seem
odd if I preferred to spend my wedding night talking on the
phone with my family instead of alone with my bride."

The insinuation of what most newly married couples
would be doing on their first night as husband and wife
wound through her, tensing her muscles, shortening her
breath, quickening her pulse.

She was attracted to Adam. Despite his alleged woman-
izing ways. Despite the fact that he was using her. Despite
the temporary nature of this relationship. She'd believed it
would be easy to ignore the chemistry for two years.

Wrong.

Forget the tea. She needed distance and solitude not a hot
drink. And she needed to get her head together and her
hormones under control. "Is it safe to walk on the beach here
at night?"

"Probably not alone."

"Oh." Another escape route sealed and another bout of
claustrophobia encroached. "Never mind then."

"Grab a jacket."

"But—"

"Lauryn. Grab a jacket. We'll walk." The words were an
order, but also a warning. One she didn't dare ignore.

Not if she wanted to get through this night without doing
something she'd regret.

Like consummating her marriage of convenience.

Six

Adam couldn't sleep.

No surprise.

He braced his forearms on the porch railing spanning the rear of the cottage and stared blindly into the night. The steady crash of the waves failed to soothe him, and the brisk sea breeze did nothing to cool his overheated skin. The woman sleeping on the other side of the closed glass doors behind him took a lot of the credit—or blame—for that.

Lauryn's kiss after the "I dos" had zapped him like an electric eel and then she'd turned off that sexual current like a circuit breaker.

How did she do it? Because he sure as hell hadn't been able to. His body still hummed.

Why now? Why her? Why did his hibernating libido have to jolt awake for a woman who wanted nothing to do with him?

It wasn't until after she had retired to her bedroom for the night that he'd realized he hadn't learned anything new about her during the long walk on the beach or the Scrabble game afterward except that she had a bigger vocabulary than he did and a competitive streak to rival his.

His wife played her cards close to her chest.

His *wife*.

Married. *Him*.

His mouth dried. He reached for his Kalik beer. The sparkle of moonlight on his wedding ring stopped him short of the bottle. He flexed his fingers, noting he didn't feel as trapped or freaked out as he'd expected.

Did he have it in him to be faithful to one woman even temporarily? God knows he'd never found a woman he wanted exclusively or one who'd seemed capable of fidelity to him. The women who came and went at Estate changed men as often as they changed clothes.

Two years with only Lauryn. One hundred four weeks. Seven hundred thirty days. And nights.

And no guarantee he'd get between her sheets.

Was infidelity encoded in DNA? If he ever fell in love, would he betray the woman the way his father had his mother? Nah, because he wasn't falling. He'd seen too many relationships turn acrimonious to ever want to go there. And knowing his father's secret and not being able to tell had been its own kind of hell.

He lifted the bottle and sipped. The Bahamas brew wasn't bad. Maybe he should check into ordering it for the club.

He couldn't check into the customs regulations tonight, but there was one decision he could make. Should he stay on the island until Monday as planned and risk driving himself nuts with need for his bride or return home early to the safety and separation a ten-thousand-square-foot house would allow?

An early return meant a command performance at the family's Sunday dinner—an event he'd prefer to postpone as long as possible. The Garrisons weren't a warm, fuzzy bunch. Scaring Lauryn off so soon in the game wouldn't be good.

They needed this honeymoon for a number of reasons.

One: appearances. A real newlywed couple would want solitude.

Two: he could hardly show up at dinner knowing nothing about the woman he'd married. If he did this charade would sink faster than lead.

Three: Lauryn jumped each time he touched her and, other than that wedding shocker, she still stiffened when he kissed her. That stung. Women didn't flinch from him. They melted, begged and wrapped themselves around him like a spider web.

But not Lauryn Lowes. Garrison. Lauryn *Garrison*.

Why not? What flipped her switches? And why didn't she desire him? Women wanted him. His bride shouldn't be an exception.

Changing her mind on the sex issue wasn't just about getting laid anymore. It was a matter of keeping the pretense. And pride. Staying in the Bahamas would give him time to diagnose and rectify the problem. He could hardly seduce her with work and family interrupting.

He needed a strategy.

The door opened behind him. Adam turned and almost choked on his beer. Lauryn stood framed in the doorway, a bedside lamp outlining her boxers-and-baggy-T-shirt-clad shape. A thin, worn T-shirt clearly outlined her full breasts and erect nipples in the pale moonlight.

He couldn't stifle a groan.

She startled and jerked to a halt. Her eyes found him in the shadows and widened. "Oh. I'm sorry. I didn't know you were out here."

"Can't sleep?"

"Um, no. You?"

"I'm used to being up nights."

"Are you hungry? I could fix something."

"Thanks, but you don't have to cook for me. I didn't marry you to get a maid or a chef."

"The estate is fully staffed?"

"Yes. And they've been informed that we're moving in."

"Can you trust them not to leak our separate sleeping arrangements?"

The muscles in the back of his neck knotted. Another reason to talk Lauryn into bed. "Good question. Like you, they signed confidentiality agreements, and they've done well with the visiting celebrities thus far. But there are no guarantees."

Her teeth gleamed in the moonlight as she bit her lip, reminding him of her taste and making him hunger for another sample. "Does the house have any suites with adjoining rooms?"

It took a second to pull his brain out of his pants. "The master suite has an attached sitting room."

"There's our solution. I'll tell them I sleep alone because you snore."

He snapped upright. "I don't snore."

She smiled, the first genuine smile she'd offered him since this *thing* began, and her eyes sparkled with mischief. The combo knocked the wind out of him and drained the blood from his brain. "I didn't say you did. I said we'd *tell* them you did."

"Why don't we tell them *you* snore?"

She shook her head. "Be a gentleman, Adam."

He'd never felt less like a gentleman in his life. He wanted to back her into that room, toss her on the bed and spend the rest of the night making her moan, beg and scream his name.

Jeezus, where did that come from?

She took a quick step backward.

Surely his wife wasn't a mind reader? Or had his lust shown on his face? "Lauryn, you don't have to leave. The deck is sturdy enough to hold both of us. We'll think of something to tell the staff—but not that I snore."

A man had his pride.

Her cautious gaze roamed over him and his recently awakened libido reacted as if her hands had done the exploring—a fact his swim trunks wouldn't be able to hide much longer. He shifted his stance. "Want a beer?"

She shook her head. "No, thank you. Were you, um, going for a swim?"

"Thought about it. But I don't know the area and forgot to ask Cassie if it was safe to swim off shore."

"Shark bait wouldn't fill the council seat." The teasing lilt of her voice zapped him with another jolt of arousal. He hadn't known she had a sense of humor.

"No, but it'd make you a rich widow."

Her amusement vanished. "Don't. Don't joke about that."

He shrugged off the concern in her voice. "So why can't you sleep?"

Please say it's because you're horny.

She eased closer to the railing, but kept a couple of yards between them. His tongue nearly fell out of his mouth at the sight of her long legs beneath those short shorts. How had he missed those legs? Had his head been stuck in a hole these past seven months?

"I kept thinking about your family. Are you comfortable deceiving them?"

Not what he wanted to hear. But maybe she was working her way up to the right answer. A man could hope. "It's necessary."

She wanted more, but he wasn't going to tell her about his quest for a larger role in Garrison, Inc. Telling her his family didn't trust him with responsibility wouldn't win her over.

He finished his beer and faced her. "We have a problem."

One golden eyebrow lifted, and so did the lush fullness of her breasts when she reached up to capture her wind-tossed hair in her hands.

"You flinch every time I touch you. My family, particularly my sisters, will pick up on that immediately."

She snatched an audible breath. "I'll work on it."

"We could practice."

A wary, caged light entered her eyes. "Practice?"

"You have a better idea?"

Her low chuckle danced over his skin like dusting fingertips. "You're beginning to sound like a corny character in a bad novel."

"Corny? *Corny?* Me?" No one had ever accused him of that. Loner, risk-taker, ambitious, emotionally unavailable? Sure. His brothers, five and six years older than him, had always dumped Adam in the same category as their younger sisters or ignored him completely. But nobody had ever called him corny.

He didn't like it. Especially not from Lauryn.

"Adam, this isn't junior high or high school where you make out just to see how far you can go before getting caught."

"You made out in junior high?"

She gave him a get-real stare.

Right. She wasn't the type. She was too…what was the word he needed? Prim? Proper? Straightlaced? And that was why she was the perfect bride for him. The council and his family had to believe he'd mended his partying ways.

"I don't do casual sex."

He moved closer, close enough to feel her body heat and catch her scent. "What's casual about sleeping with your husband?"

Her throat moved as she swallowed and awareness tightened her face. Sexual tension crackled in the air around them. "L-let me rephrase that. I don't do meaningless sex. And you agreed. To the no-sex clause."

"Then what do you suggest?" He lifted a hand to smooth her hair, but she flinched out of reach.

"Can't we just be…friends?"

"Friends." The last thing any guy wants to hear from a woman.

He'd never survive four days in paradise with his reluctant bride without losing his mind. And the thought of two years of celibacy made his package shrivel.

He had to come up with a plan. A plan to seduce his wife.

Lauryn wasn't ready for this. Not yet.

Who was she kidding? She'd *never* be ready to try and convince the people who knew Adam best that she was head over heels in love with him. But she'd try. That was their deal.

She clung tightly to Adam's hand as they approached the Garrisons' Bal Harbor estate on Sunday night and hoped she didn't blow it.

She would have preferred staying in the Bahamas and tiptoeing around the growing sexual tension between her and Adam to meeting his family *en masse,* but this morning he'd suddenly insisted on coming home early to organize the move and have Sunday dinner with his family. They'd spent most of the day apart in their respective homes packing boxes for the movers to pick up tomorrow. But that brief reprieve was over and now the spotlight was on her and she had a touch of stage fright.

Knowing she'd be sleeping in Adam's condo tonight didn't help her anxiety level, but the house wasn't ready. Specifically, the sofa bed for the sitting room wouldn't be delivered until tomorrow morning. Since she'd refused to let Adam share her bed and he'd refused to sleep in another room for one night, the condo had been their only option.

Lauryn was so nervous she was almost nauseous. She searched her mind for a distraction. "Mrs. Suarez said something about your brothers getting married recently?"

Adam didn't slow his pace as he crossed the brick driveway. "Parker married Anna, his executive assistant, in August. Stephen married Megan in September, and they have a three-year-old daughter who probably won't be here tonight. My sister Brittany is engaged to Emilio Jefferies, one of Garrison, Inc.'s rivals. If he's here, you can expect Parker to be on his worst behavior. Brooke is still single."

"How will I tell the twins apart?"

"Brooke is a people-pleaser. Count on Mother to be yanking her chain. Brittany is more laid-back."

"And your brothers?"

"Parker's the oldest and he's a control freak. Stephen's okay."

Control freak? Was there tension between Adam and his brother? "Will Cassie and Brandon be here?"

"Not likely."

"That's too bad." Lauryn could have used a friendly face.

"Trust me, it's better to keep Mother and Cassie apart."

Cassie would be a reminder of Mr. Garrison's infidelity. That wouldn't be easy for any woman to take. "I guess so. I wasn't thinking."

The setting sun cast a mellow light over the creamy stucco walls and terracotta tile roof of an imposing Spanish-style house. If Lauryn weren't meeting her in-laws she'd probably find the place attractive in a grandiose we-have-loads-of-money way.

And then it hit her and she almost tripped. She'd married a millionaire. Sure, she'd known Adam came from the same affluent community her mother had, but Lauryn had never made the connection that *she* had married money and soon she'd be living like this. Probably because the money aspect wasn't what mattered. She wanted those diaries. She had no interest in being showered with diamonds and no desire to be a pampered, kept woman. No matter what Adam wanted.

When this was over she'd go back to life as usual, albeit with an extremely nice nest egg.

Adam stopped in front of the mahogany door and hit her with a head-on gaze. "You look beautiful. Remind me to thank Cassie for that dress."

Pleasure rushed through her. "I chose it."

"Very nice. Conservative and tasteful, but with a latent sexuality that any man would enjoy tapping. Remember, don't flinch," he whispered as he cradled her cheek in a warm palm and then he covered her mouth with his. Lauryn didn't have time to react—or not—to the unexpected kiss before the front door opened. Adam slowly lifted his head.

His hand lingered on her jaw line before he released her and then he flashed a disarmingly boyish and guilty grin at the fiftyish-year-old woman inside. "Late again. I know. But I was distracted."

The woman's stern face melted into a smile. "Well, you're here now. Come in. You know what happens when you keep her waiting."

Her? Who?

Adam tugged Lauryn forward. "Lauryn, this is Lisette Wilson. She's the saint who manages my mother. Lisette, meet my beautiful bride, Lauryn."

"So you really did it?" a male voice called from inside.

Lisette quickly shook Lauryn's hand, greeting her warmly and then stepping aside.

A tall, dark-haired, brown-eyed man stood behind her.

Adam ushered Lauryn inside a foyer almost as large as Lauryn's living room. "Ask Brandon and Cassie. They were our witnesses. Lauryn, my brother Stephen."

Stephen appraised Lauryn as he shook her hand, and then turned to an approaching man who looked uncannily like him. Same hair, eyes and a similar build. Definitely a Garrison even though neither man shared Adam's sexy blue eyes. "Pay up."

"The one digging for his wallet is Parker," Adam said dryly. "I can't believe you guys bet on my wedding."

Stephen shrugged. "What can I say? You are the last one anyone thought would settle down. But hey, I bet you would. Eventually."

"This is Lauryn. You might have seen her around Estate. She's the only woman I let play with my…accounts." Adam flashed a teasing smile and wink her way for the benefit of their audience, and Lauryn nearly swallowed her tongue. Adam deserved a standing ovation for his acting ability.

Five more people crowded into the foyer practically forcing Lauryn and Adam against the door and increasing Lauryn's sense of being trapped. She easily identified the two slender brunettes as the twins. Another dark-haired woman, a redhead and an olive-complexioned man made up the group. The names blurred as Lauryn shook hands and accepted what seemed to be genuine welcomes.

This isn't so bad.

"Adam, I never expected you to literally take my advice and settle down," one of the twins said. Brittany, Lauryn decided, because she held hands with the only non-Garrison male. Emilio.

"You mean my advice," Stephen corrected and his sister rolled her eyes. Stephen gravitated toward the redhead. Megan?

Adam's arm slid around Lauryn's waist. For once she was glad to have him to lean on and burrowed tighter against his side. She saw the surprise and the flare of arousal in his eyes as he looked down at her. She hoped he remembered she was acting. "Neither of you get credit. I found Lauryn without your help."

"May I see your ring?" Brooke asked.

With all eyes focused on her Lauryn wanted to squirm. She extended her hand and hoped it didn't tremble too much.

"It's beautiful."

"Your brother has excellent taste." Good. Her voice sounded almost normal.

Brooke looked doubtful. "Adam does? How long have you been dating?"

Panic hit Lauryn hard and fast. She and Adam hadn't discussed that. She looked at him but he'd turned to talk to Stephen. "Um, not long. We met when I interviewed for the job at Estate seven and a half months ago, but we, um, tried to deny our feelings…because of the no-fraternization policy."

She stuck to the truth as much as she could because she hated lying to these people. To anyone, really. She'd spent too much of her youth telling whoppers. And getting caught. She kept waiting for the half-truths of her current life to blow up in her face. One misstep and—

"What is wrong with you people?" a harsh and slightly slurred female voice asked from behind the others. The group parted for the thin woman barging through them like a Coast Guard cutter. Her short dark hair was streaked with gray. Her cold, blue gaze plowed into Lauryn's. Adam's eyes, only

Lauryn had never seen his look as hard. And she hoped she never did.

"Why is it none of my children have the decency to marry in a church?"

"Hello, Mother," Adam said.

The chilly gaze raked Lauryn from head to toe before shifting to Adam. He air-kissed his mother's cheek with about as much warmth as a polar ice cap. "This is Lauryn. My wife."

"So I hear."

Lauryn suppressed a flinch at the caustic tone.

Adam continued as if his mother hadn't rudely interrupted. "Lauryn, Bonita Garrison. My mother."

"It's nice to meet—"

"Are you pregnant?" Bonita Garrison snarled.

Lauryn gasped and lowered the hand she'd extended. "No."

"Good. I need another drink. Lisette!" Adam's mother wheeled around and headed across the vast living room beyond a fat stone column. The housekeeper hustled after her.

"I shouldn't be surprised to find her already working her way through a bottle," Adam muttered.

"That's our mother," Brittany said. "I can't believe you didn't take Lauryn on a decent honeymoon. Three days in the Bahamas? Please. I never took you for a cheapskate."

Adam shrugged. "We have too much to do. We're moving into the Sunset Island estate tomorrow. I'll make it up to Lauryn later."

"You're giving up the bachelor pad?" Stephen said in a surprise-laden voice.

"No. The property's too valuable to sell and it should continue to appreciate. The club will use it the same way I've been using the estate. But Lauryn and I want a home. The kind you'd raise a family in." He quoted her words from the night he'd given her the house tour.

Adam's arm around Lauryn's waist guided her along with the group as it moved toward the French doors on the far side of the room, through which Bonita Garrison had disappeared. Outside, a limestone patio surrounded an Olympic-size pool. A border of tall palms swayed in the evening breeze. Lauryn tried not to gawk, but it was impossible not to be overwhelmed by such opulence.

"Drink?" Adam released her and moved toward a marble-topped wet bar.

Lauryn debated sipping something to calm her nerves versus the possibility of loosening her tongue and tripping over it. And then she noticed Adam's disconcerted expression. She realized he had no clue of her drink preference. "Um, sure. Do you have a dry white wine tonight?"

"Coming up."

"We're late for dinner," Mrs. Garrison groused.

Adam leisurely reached for a goblet and bottle. "Go ahead, Mother. Lauryn and I will join you in a minute. Lisette, would you ask the kitchen to serve champagne with dessert? And join us for a glass."

The housekeeper flushed. "My pleasure, Mr. Adam."

His mother flounced off, leaving her children looking after her with almost identical looks of disgust on their faces.

When Adam handed Lauryn the wineglass, she considered knocking it back in one gulp. Adam obviously shared the sentiment since he downed half his bourbon in one swallow.

"You don't have to wait for us," Adam said and the others filed inside, but Adam caught her elbow and held her back.

"Is something wrong?" she asked.

"Just doing what's expected." He encircled her waist, pulled her close and kissed her. Taking advantage of her surprised "Oh," he skipped the preliminaries and deepened the kiss. She tasted the liquor on his tongue, but it wasn't unpleasant. Neither was the warmth of his body against hers.

She dug the fingers of her free hand into his firm waist and struggled to shut down her knee-weakening, nerve-tingling response to his scent, his heat, the skill of the silken tongue plying hers. But denying the sexual heat he generated wasn't possible. He made all her senses come alive in ways beyond the hot rush of sex she remembered from her wilder days. She yearned to burrow closer, to linger and explore.

What would it be like to be Adam's lover? Would the intimate act live up to the promise in his kisses or would he disappoint her as others had before him?

Don't start liking this.

Too late.

When he finally lifted his head she panted as if she'd run a mile. She licked her sensitized lips and tried to quell her clamoring hormones and catch her breath. "W-why did you do that?"

"We're being watched," he said against her neck. He caught her face when she would have turned and traced the shell of her ear with a featherlight touch. "Don't look."

His five-o'clock shadow rasped deliciously against her skin as he nuzzled from behind her ear to her collarbone, his breath warm and moist. She shivered. Just when she thought she'd dissolve into a wet puddle on the patio tiles he slowly straightened and released her. A dark flush coated his cheekbones.

"If you're ready for battle, let's go."

Lauryn's stomach plunged and she nearly dropped her wineglass. Any lingering remnants of desire vanished. "It gets worse?"

"Usually. Garrison family dinners are not enjoyed. They're endured."

"Then why do you come?"

"Because they're my family." Adam laced his fingers through hers and, palm-to-palm, led her toward what felt increasingly like the lion's den.

And then she remembered her father's favorite quote. "There's a price for every lie you tell. Before you open your mouth, be sure you're prepared to pay it."

The tension throughout dinner was of the clichéd thick-enough-to-cut-with-a-knife variety.

Beneath the superficially polite conversation Lauryn sensed undercurrents between the members of the Garrison clan, but especially between Parker and his soon-to-be brother-in-law, Emilio Jeffries. She'd have to ask Adam to explain the family dynamics later. But for now she was glad the ordeal was almost over. The staff had served the dessert, poured the champagne and left the room.

"Anna's pregnant," Parker announced.

Lauryn lifted her gaze to the brunette sitting directly across from her. "Congratulations."

Anna's eyes shone with happiness. "Thank you. You can see why I for one would have been thrilled if you were pregnant. We could have compared notes."

Lauryn ignored the derisive snort from Bonita and shifted in her chair. "Sorry."

"Perhaps soon," Adam said. He captured Lauryn's hand and carried it to his lips for a tender kiss topped off with one of those charismatic smiles that made her heart flutter irregularly. "I'd like to make a toast to my beautiful bride, the only woman to ever make 'forever' sound like a promise instead of a life sentence."

Lauryn almost knocked over her stemware. She had to remind herself Adam was acting, and that she had no reason whatsoever to turn warm and mushy when he looked at her that way.

"Here, here," and "Congratulations," echoed around the table. Adam leaned forward and whispered a kiss across her lips.

He was good. Very good. And she almost regretted him drawing back. Their gazes remained locked and tendrils of need spiraled through her.

He's your husband. Sex with him would be okay.

No, it wouldn't. You don't love him and he doesn't love you. Wait for someone who matters. Someone who cares about you and not just about getting off.

But she wanted him. More than she could ever remember wanting anyone.

"Well, since we're making announcements…" Brooke's hesitant statement startled Lauryn back into awareness of her surroundings. She blinked and looked away from Adam's mesmerizing blue eyes. Brooke paused, inhaled deeply and then said in a rush, "I'm pregnant, too."

Shocked silence filled the room, and then Bonita barked, "By whom?"

"I'm sorry, Mother, that's none of your business."

"It is my business if you are going to shame this family like your father with another bastard," Bonita bit out.

Lauryn winced, thinking of Cassie. No, her new friend definitely wouldn't be welcome here.

"Who's the father, Brooke?" Adam sounded fierce. Angry. Protective. Lauryn filed that surprising facet to her new husband away.

"I'm a grown woman, Adam. I don't need my brothers to fight my battles for me. Suffice to say, the father is not going to be a part of my baby's life or mine and leave it at that."

Bonita slammed her glass on the table, sloshing half the clear liquid—she'd refused the champagne—onto the damask cloth. The smell of gin filled the air. "Don't expect Garrison money to support your mistake."

She rose unsteadily and left the dining room in a huff with Lisette hot on her heels.

Adam broke the uneasy silence. "Brooke, how are you going to manage the condo complex and take care of the baby alone? The bastard responsible should help—at least financially."

His sister's chin lifted. "I don't want his help, and I'll have day care or a nanny like any other parent."

"What about maternity leave?" Brittany asked quietly.

Brooke looked at the faces around table. "Look, I'm not saying I have all the details worked out. This was a surprise for me, too. But I am having this baby with or without my family's support. Now can we *please* talk about something else?"

Lauryn could feel Adam's tension across the space between them, and she was touched by his need to charge to his sister's aid, but now wasn't the time. Brooke looked too on edge.

Lauryn covered the hand fisted in Adam's lap to draw his attention. When he met her gaze, she silently urged him to change the subject. He inclined his head slightly and turned back to his siblings.

"We have to do something about Mother's drinking. It was bad before, but it's worsened since Dad died."

Lauryn noticed Brooke looked relieved by the diversion.

"What do you suggest?" Parker asked. "Locking the liquor cabinet? It won't work."

"What about rehab?" Megan, Stephen's wife, suggested.

Adam's hand fisted on the table. "It's our best shot. She's not going to quit on her own."

"She's not going to go to rehab voluntarily, either," Brittany added.

"Tough." At that moment Lauryn thought Adam looked hard enough to force his mother into capitulating—as hard as his mother had looked at Lauryn earlier.

A frisson of unease slithered up her spine. Adam wouldn't make a good adversary.

Several tense, silent moments passed, and then Brittany cleared her throat. "On a positive note, Emilio and I plan to get married at Christmas. We'd like you all to be there."

Parker scowled at Emilio and then shifted his attention to his sister. "Is that wise considering we have a spy within Garrison, Inc. feeding information to your fiancé's family?"

"Dammit, Parker," Emilio growled, "Jordan does not have a spy in your company."

"How can you be certain when you've admitted you and Jordan aren't on speaking terms?"

"I could look into it," Adam offered.

"Forget it. I'll handle it," Parker snapped back.

"You're not handling it," Adam insisted. "The information leak has been going on for months. A fresh set of eyes—"

"I said, I'll handle it."

Adam persisted, "I want to help, and I'm more persuasive than you."

"Forget it, *little brother*. We're not talking about charming the panties off women. This is business."

Lauryn's cheeks burned with embarrassment. *She* was one of the women Adam had supposedly charmed out of her clothing.

Adam turned rigid beside her. The men looked ready to come to blows. Lauryn rested a hand on Adam's forearm and then glared at Parker. "You shouldn't dismiss Adam's business acumen. Estate is extremely profitable because of him, and the employee turnover rate is next to nil. He knows what he's doing and he knows how to read and manage people."

All eyes turned on her.

Her stomach sank. Good grief. She'd reacted like one of Pavlov's dogs again with another conditioned response. Why had she opened her mouth? Because Parker's insulting tone hit one of her hot buttons. But this was not her fight and arguing wasn't the way to make a good impression with the in-laws.

Parker drilled her with an unblinking stare—nothing new to Lauryn since her father used to do the same—and when she didn't cower or look away he scanned the rest of the party.

"I don't need Adam's help because I'm looking into brokering a deal with Jordan Jefferies just to keep the peace between our families."

Almost everyone at the table gaped at Parker in surprise…everyone except Brooke, who looked relieved, probably because her pregnancy was no longer the topic of conversation. Lauryn glanced at Adam and found him watching his sister with a frown puckering his brow.

Lauryn only half listened while Parker outlined the potential deal.

Something very important had just happened at this table. And it wasn't Parker's announcement.

And then she remembered the research she'd done for a college psychology paper. She'd been fascinated by the way birth order affected personality and behavior—mainly because she'd needed to understand her own twisted family dynamics and her hackles-raised response to her father's edicts.

If she remembered correctly, the textbooks said middle children often reported feeling invisible and overlooked. It wasn't unusual for them to seek recognition.

She studied her husband.

Gulp. Her *husband.*

Adam seemed far too confident to need anyone's approval—other than the business council's nominating committee, that is. He'd claimed it wasn't the council presidency that mattered, but what it represented.

She fingered her champagne glass. What did that position of responsibility represent?

Recognition of his success from the Miami business community?

Or respect from his family?

Seven

Lauryn had defended him tonight.

Adam couldn't remember the last time someone had stepped up to the plate for him. Not his father, his mother or his brothers. He didn't expect his sisters to because as the older sibling it was his job to look out for Brooke and Britt.

And yet Lauryn had gone to bat for him without hesitation and without him asking her to. That flash of fire in her eyes when she'd stared Parker down had been downright sexy. It made Adam desire her even more.

Would she be as passionate a lover?

With his thoughts fixated on the woman making use of his bathroom, he sat on his bed in his loft bedroom staring blindly at the half wall that overlooked the living room below. Lauryn wasn't the first female to shower here by a long shot, but she was the only one who'd ever made him want to pull up a chair and watch the water stream over her

naked curves. Better yet, join her and let his hands and
mouth follow the water's path.

*That's because by the time a woman uses your shower
you've already had her, and you're eager to put her into a
cab and send her home.*

His women didn't sleep here. Lauryn would be the first.

Moments later the bathroom door opened and Lauryn
emerged in a cloud of steam. She'd pinned up her hair, but
damp tendrils clung to her freshly scrubbed and flushed
cheeks.

How could he have ever believed her mousy? She looked
so damned desirable wearing the shapeless baggy shorts and
worn T-shirt his teeth ached.

"Why did you defend me tonight?"

She jerked to a halt and hugged the black dress she'd
worn to dinner tighter against her chest. The garment had
covered her from neck to knees, outlining an hourglass shape
that made his mouth water and his hands itch to explore. The
sexy little slit in the back hem of the skirt had had him
groaning at each glimpse of thigh. He saw more skin on the
Estate dance floor every night, but because Lauryn dressed
conservatively, that flash of taboo territory had hit him like
a bouncer's taser.

She shifted her weight from one long, lean leg to the other.
"Something in your brother's condescending tone ticked me
off. He reminded me of—"

She mashed her lips together and shook her head as if re-
gretting her words and headed toward the dresser.

He rose, blocking her path and putting them face-to-face
with barely a foot between them. "Of who?"

She tipped her head back, met his gaze and then sighed.
"Of my father. He was a control freak, too. Very his-way-or-
the-highway."

The thought of Lauryn being browbeaten into submission lit a bonfire of anger in Adam's belly. Was that why she was so conservative and quiet now?

"Lauryn, I don't need you to fight my battles for me," he said softly.

"I'm sure you don't." She ducked around him, tossed her dress over the back of his valet chair, and then with her back to him, dug around in her suitcase as if she'd find buried treasure inside.

Adam crossed the loft, stopping behind her. Her scent filled his nostrils and her warmth drew him like a fire does a shipwrecked sailor. He rested one hand on her hip and traced a damp lock clinging to her nape with the other.

She stiffened, but not soon enough to still feel her tremor.

"I don't need your defense, but I appreciate it," he said against her ear.

"It's what a wife would do, isn't it?" she asked without moving.

"No clue. I'm flying blind here."

She slowly turned. He detected a flicker of hunger in her eyes and his lungs jammed.

"Adam… You laid it on a bit thick tonight. I know making your family believe this is real is—"

"You kissed me back. On the beach. By the pool. In the driveway."

Her expression turned wary. "Maybe I'm as good an actor as you."

"You can't fake the arousal darkening your cheeks or widening your pupils." He lowered his eyes to the stiff nipples tenting her shirt. "You can't fake that."

She folded her arms and lifted her chin. "And your point is…?"

"You want me."

"Me and a hundred other women. But part of being an adult is realizing you can't have everything you want."

He spread his arms. "You can have me. Any way you want me."

She hesitated for a moment, catching her bottom lip with her teeth and then her mouth twisted in a wry grimace. "So I've heard."

Not the invitation to share the only bed in the condo he'd been hoping for. "Is that what this is about? You're waiting for the blood test results?"

"No. I'm adhering to our agreement."

At some time during the miserable family dinner he'd forgotten about convincing his siblings he'd settled down, and he'd started looking for excuses to touch Lauryn, to make her breath catch, her skin flush. He'd actively sought opportunities to kiss her because kissing her filled him with an excitement and anticipation he hadn't felt for anyone or anything in a very long time.

How many kisses had he stolen tonight? Four? No, five. After that last one by the car he'd been so hard he could barely fold himself into the Beemer to drive them home.

"Agreements can be amended." He cupped her nape, savoring the warm silkiness of her skin against his palm. "Let me show you how good it could be between us, Lauryn."

Her lids fluttered closed, and then she sucked a quick breath and popped them open again. "No."

It wasn't as if he'd never heard "no" before, but he'd never heard it from a woman who'd almost eaten him alive on three separate occasions. He could accept Lauryn's refusal and walk away if she didn't want him. But she did.

So why the mixed signals? Why make them both suffer? He wanted to kiss her until she begged him to peel off her clothing, toss her onto his king-size bed and bury himself in her wet heat.

He'd bet she'd be as hot as her mouth.

No. Hotter. Wetter. He broke a sweat just thinking about it.

As if she'd read his mind her eyes widened, her lips parted on an unsteady inhalation and color washed her face and neck, warming the skin beneath his hand.

Oh yeah. She wanted him. He pulled her forward.

"Your family's approval," she blurted when he was an inch from her delectable mouth. Her palms spread on his chest and pushed. "That's why you want to win the business council's nomination. Isn't it?"

Talk about a mood-killer. He straightened and released her. "That's personal."

"So you keep saying. But, Adam, the day I became your wife I became part of your personal life. If you don't tell me what's going on I can't help."

He wasn't going to get laid tonight. Unless he changed her mind he'd be sleeping downstairs on the sofa.

Shoving a hand through his hair, he turned and walked toward the half wall and braced his arms on the ledge. He debated how much to reveal. But like she'd said, she was part of this now. "I want a bigger stake in Garrison, Inc."

"Why? Isn't Estate enough?"

"No. It's not. My father kept me out of the Garrison offices when he was alive and now Parker's doing the same. And I'm sick of having to prove myself only to be denied an equal share in the family business."

She joined him by the rail. "But why does that matter? You're successful without Parker's approval."

"I don't want his approval." His frustrated growl sent her eyebrows skyward. "I was groomed to take my place in the family business. I have the education and experience to take a more active role. I can't help wondering if I was denied a place at Garrison, Inc. because I knew about my father's affair with Cassie's mother and had the balls to call him on it."

"You think you're being punished because you didn't keep quiet and take one for the team?"

"Exactly. But I'll never know. Will I?"

"You do realize you're not being kept out because you lack business acumen, don't you? I wasn't lying when I told Parker you run a first-rate organization. I've worked in several places that weren't, so I know what I'm talking about."

Her support expanded something inside his chest.

She tilted her head and considered him in silence for several moments. "You're a typical middle child, you know."

"What does that mean?" And was it an insult?

"Middle children have to find their own niche, their own way to excel, to stand out from the crowd."

"That's…accurate. Parker and Stephen were always tight with each other and with our father. Brooke and Brittany had the girl thing going. I learned early on to entertain myself and go after what I wanted. Alone. If I wanted my parents' attention I had to do something grander, wilder or louder than my siblings. In the process I earned a reckless reputation I can't seem to live down even though I quit that juvenile behavior years ago."

"And you think having a wife will help you shake the bad rep?"

"The right kind of wife, yes."

She wrapped her arms around her middle and turned toward the two-story window wall opposite the loft. He followed her gaze. The lights of a cruise ship leaving the Port of Miami via Government Cut twinkled against the night sky.

The ocean view had been a prime draw in his purchase of the condo. But the view couldn't soothe him tonight.

He looked into her eyes. "You're an only child?"

"Yes."

"And what are typical onlies like?"

Lauryn shifted, glanced away. "Onlies can go one of two ways. Conformist or rebel."

"Which were you?"

Her cautious gaze found his again. "Which do you think?"

He considered her conventional clothing, her restrained hair and body language and her solitary life. "Conformist. Which is a good thing since a woman with a wild reputation is the last thing I need."

And yet the urge to make her wild *in bed* had him aroused to the verge of wanting to say to hell with his no-sex promise. He turned abruptly, crossed the loft and yanked back the comforter. "Let's hit the sack."

She remained by the railing. "I told you I'm not sharing your bed."

"Lauryn, there's only one bed. Since we're moving to the estate tomorrow, I didn't convert the study into a bedroom."

"If I were willing to share then we'd be staying at the Sunset Island estate tonight. I'll take the sofa. Do you have a spare pillow?"

"What's the matter? Don't trust yourself not to jump me?"

Another long stretch of silence filled the air before she averted her gaze. "Maybe."

Her honesty hit him like a sucker punch.

But he wasn't sure he could control himself if she was in bed beside him, either. As badly as he craved her body, he wasn't taking her until she was wet, willing and begging.

Until then, he could survive a few sleepless nights. "Take the bed."

* * *

Lauryn's pulse raced and her palms dampened. Standing at the top of the stairs of the Sunset estate, she weighed her choices.

Three hallways radiated off the balcony encircling the foyer like the points of the mariner's compass inlaid in the foyer floor below. Left? Right? Dead ahead? Which hall led to her birthmother's bedroom?

Downstairs Adam closed the front door behind the departing movers. He'd insisted on emptying her apartment, and the crew had stored most of her furniture and belongings in an empty staff apartment above one of the garages. They'd left her and Adam's suitcases in the foyer.

She heard Adam's tread on the stairs and turned to watch him ascend. Worn jeans and a white T-shirt fit him like a second skin, outlining a body worthy of a pin-up calendar. His biceps bulged under the weight of her overstuffed luggage.

Sexy. Her mouth dried. *But just sex isn't enough anymore. Remember? No more meaningless affairs. You promised.*

But promises couldn't prevent the fine hairs on her body from rising like antennae whenever he was near. She'd never been so aware—so *constantly, completely* aware—of anyone before. And the more she found out about him, the worse her fascination became.

"Found the master suite yet?" he asked as he reached her side.

"Um, no." Her feet had refused to carry her beyond the landing. Now that she was where she'd longed to be for the better part of a year, she was afraid she'd discover this was nothing but a wild-goose chase and the diaries weren't here.

But what if they were? She didn't doubt the outcome—whichever it might be—would change her life. And maybe not for the better.

He tilted his head. "This way."

She followed Adam down the wide center hall toward the back of the house. Her gaze dropped from his broad shoulders to his butt doing a fine job of filling out his jeans.

Control yourself, for pity's sake.

"Our room is over the sunroom downstairs. It's the newest part of the house, added about fifteen years ago."

Before her mother died.

He went through a pair of double doors. A twenty-foot hall led her past a walk-in closet as large as her apartment living room with drawers built into a center island. Adam paused long enough to set her luggage down inside the door and then continued down the hall. Next they passed a bathroom that looked like something out of *Architectural Digest*. White marble floors. A round glass shower stall. A decadent, oversize sunken tub. Enough black marble counter space to fill a kitchen. Opposite the bathroom, an open third door revealed a comfortable-looking sitting room and the new sofa bed. Is that where she'd sleep?

She followed Adam into the sun-filled, semicircular bedroom decorated in beachy colors of sand, pearl, apricot and periwinkle. A massive raised platform bed sat against the interior wall. Its carved scallop-shaped headboard had been painted to resemble the opalescent inside of a shell. The curved exterior walls were all windows like the sunroom downstairs and shared the same view of the pool, dock and tennis courts. A chaise, love seat and small bistro table with a pair of chairs offered perfect places to share coffee or curl up and read a book.

"It's beautiful, and the view is amazing, but there's not much privacy, is there? Anyone looking out the back windows of the house can see what we're doing in here."

"One button closes the curtains." Adam flipped a switch

and a nearly silent motor closed the drapes, darkening the room completely and sealing them in shadowy seclusion. Before her eyes could adjust he hit the switch again and the curtains reopened.

The suite was much smaller than the beach house and much more intimate than his condo. Could she share this space and not give in to the sexual urges rising within her like a tidal surge?

An image flashed in her mind—an image that had haunted her all day. She tried and failed to erase it. This morning she'd awoken before Adam and tiptoed to the loft rail to see him sprawled on the sofa just below his bedroom. The plentiful display of sleek golden skin made it clear he slept nude. She'd wasted way too much time staring down at him and hoping the sheet barely covering his groin would fall to the floor.

Voyeur. A guilty flush warmed her skin.

It's just healthy curiosity. Right?

No. It was more than that. Her early days crush was back, she realized with a sinking sensation in her stomach. And it hadn't returned because of the grand gestures like the expensive car or rings. It was the little things like how Adam had been such a great sport when she'd beat him at Scrabble, or the way he opened doors and held chairs for her and always treated her with respect even though she'd basically sold herself to him.

It was the way he worried about his sister and mother, and how he hadn't ridiculed Lauryn's fear of flying. Instead, during the flight he'd explained how the plane worked, and on the return trip to Miami he'd encouraged her to take the controls for a few minutes. When she'd admitted she liked it he'd offered to arrange flying lessons for her.

She understood his struggle with his father and sympathized with his need to live down a less-than-admirable past. They had that in common.

If she weren't married to him she'd want to date him.

Maybe Adam wasn't the womanizer the tabloids claimed. Maybe he wasn't just another guy out to get laid as often as possible.

He wasn't a guy who shirked hard work, and if he were the playboy the press claimed, he would have stood back and let the paid crew do all the sweating, but he'd worked right alongside the movers today. The scent fresh of male sweat emanated from him.

And maybe you're clutching at straws because you want him.

Adam eliminated the space between them with two long strides. He braced a hand on the window frame beside her head and leaned closer. "The bed's big enough for both of us."

She shouldn't be tempted. But she was. "Adam. We've already had this conversation."

"Lauryn," he replied in the same long-suffering tone she'd used, but laughter and an invitation to sin lurked in his gorgeous blue eyes—an invitation she wanted to accept more with each passing moment.

"You're not making this easy."

"No." He cradled her face. The warmth of his palm felt so good, and the urge to lean into his touch nearly overwhelmed her.

And that was another thing. He was honest—despite their dishonest sham of a marriage. He wanted her and he didn't try to hide that fact. It made her feel a twinge of guilt over being less than one hundred percent forthcoming with him.

He just made wanting him so damned easy.

Sleeping with him wouldn't be a desperate bid for approval or a jab to get back at your father.

But it would still be wrong. In the overall scheme of things giving in to lust would not move her toward her long-term goals, and these days she always thought of the future.

She wanted to back away, to break his hold and put a safe distance between them, but this marriage was all about appearances. Adam had asked the cook to prepare a special meal for their first night in the house. If they were going to make their separate sleeping arrangements believable, public displays of affection and even passion would be necessary. Adam must have spotted some of the staff watching through the windows.

Before she could ask if that were the case he lowered his head and covered her mouth with his. He sipped from her lips and teased with his tongue, stroking and then suckling her bottom lip. Every cell in her body snapped to attention. She loved the way he kissed. Adored the way he tasted.

Last night's kiss in his mother's driveway had been hot, but not nearly as incinerating as this one. This one was a no-holds-barred assault on her senses. Hunger rose within her like mercury in a thermometer, overriding caution, good judgment and restraint and making her crave more than just kisses.

Adam backed her against the window frame. His thigh slid between hers, pressing her tender flesh. He deepened the kiss. One big hand raked upward from her waist to cover her breast. He found the sensitive tip and brushed over it again and again. Her stomach tensed with need. His erection pressed against her belly and the heat of his torso branded hers. She curled her fingers against the urge to cup and caress his hardened flesh, to test his length and breadth.

A niggling part of her brain cried *overkill*. No one watching from outside could see his tongue twining with hers or his hand on her breast. But the rest of her body mutinied. She wanted this. Wanted him. Wanted his touch. Wanted to feel the passion she'd denied herself for so long. She moved against his thigh and bubbles of pleasure floated through her system.

He lowered his hand to cover her mound. Her khaki shorts did nothing to lessen the shocking, arousing contact. She broke the kiss to gasp for air and let her head fall back against the window frame. Adam stroked her through her clothing and a moan sneaked past her lips.

You shouldn't let him do this.

Stop him. You're too vulnerable right now to think straight.

Adam nibbled and kissed her neck while his fingers worked magic. Lauryn lost herself in the heat of his breath against her skin, the nip of his teeth along the cords of her neck, the swirl of his tongue over her pulse point. She clenched her fingers in the silkiness of his hair.

Pull.

Him.

Away.

But she couldn't. Not yet. Pleasure, heady and out of control, rose swiftly until orgasm boiled through her.

Barely able to support her weight, she clung to Adam's shoulders and sagged against the hard window frame. She forced her heavy lids open and stared into Adam's passion-darkened eyes.

"Good?" he rasped between labored breaths.

Shame burned her cheeks. She lowered her arms. "You know it was. But it shouldn't have happened."

She'd slipped up. Big-time. Embarrassed, she turned her head to look out at the empty patio below. A quick scan of the downstairs windows revealed no one watching. "We don't have an audience."

Adam straightened, steadied her and then released her. A

slow smile eased across his lips. "That was for me. I told you. I always go after what I want. And I want you, Lauryn Garrison. Consider yourself warned."

And then he winked and strolled out of the room.

Lauryn's knees gave out. She slid to the floor.

What had she done?

She'd opened Pandora's Box, that's what.

And she wasn't convinced she could put the lid back on.

She'd done it again.

Lauryn's stomach flip-flopped. She'd lost herself in the music and sent signals she hadn't intended to send to her husband—signals that said she was available and sexually interested in more than just faking a relationship.

No wonder Adam had spun her into a tight embrace on the dance floor. The heat of his chest pressed her back and his arms, one around her waist and the other just below her breasts, held her close as he swayed to the music of the Grammy Award winner singing on Estate's main stage.

Adam's lips teased the sensitive skin beneath her left ear and his arousal nudged her hips. It was the urge to push back without the barrier of clothing between them that filled Lauryn with panic.

Her reasons for resisting a physical relationship grew foggier each day. Worse, Adam knew it. She saw the knowledge in his eyes each time he looked at her, felt it in the confidence and increased frequency of his touch and the seduction of his lips. The lovey-dovey gestures were supposed to be for show, for their audience. But she knew better—especially since he was slipping a few in when there was no one around.

He seemed bent on seducing her with flowers, jewelry and a handful of other small gifts, which she found by her plate, on her pillow, on her desk. But it was the easy flow of conversation over brunch each morning that was slowly eroding her defenses.

The man knew how to woo women.

But she didn't want to be just another conquest.

She wriggled herself free and faced Adam on the crowded dance floor. She had to lean close to be heard, close enough to smell the unique scent of his body mingling with his tangy cologne. *Sexy.* Her pulse quickened.

"Would you mind if I headed home early tonight?"

Adam's brows lowered and his eyes filled with concern. He caught her elbow and led her off the floor. "Something wrong?"

Yes, something was wrong. She'd lost sight of her goal and had yet to spend any time searching closets for loose floorboards. Other than the master suite, she'd only taken a cursory walk through the upstairs. Part of that was Adam's fault. He insisted on keeping up the inseparable newlywed image and they were always together. Her only time away from him was afternoons when she worked at Estate. Even then he was only ten steps down the hall in his office.

At six each evening he drove her home to change for dinner at a see-and-be-seen restaurant where he touched her at every opportunity. Afterward they returned to the club and stayed until 3:00 a.m. More touching ensued with occasional dances thrown in. Adam's moves on the dance floor were so sexy she couldn't help but wonder what he'd be like in bed.

And now she was as hot as a downed power line.

Self-disgust welled within her. Four days of living in her birthmother's house—*four days!*—and she had nothing to show for them except a case of overactive hormones and a body clock that no longer knew the difference between night and day.

"I need to catch up on my sleep." The lie caused a pinch of guilt. She needed an empty house to do what she'd come to Florida to do.

If you were honest with Adam about your birthmother you wouldn't have to lie. Soon, she promised herself. She'd tell him soon. She liked and respected him too much to continue lying to him about her reasons for seeking him out.

"I'll walk you out."

And if he did he'd kiss her good-night. Her resistance was already running low. She needed to avoid that talented, persuasive mouth of his before it led her straight to his bed.

"No, Adam, I've already cut into the hours you usually work. Stay until the club closes like you used to."

Adam had never worried about one of his women before, but he hadn't been able to get Lauryn out of his head in the past hour.

Why had she left the club so abruptly? Was she ill?

One minute she'd been dancing so seductively he'd been rock hard and ready to drag her to his office to pick up where they'd left off the other day. The next second she'd frozen and bolted.

He'd leave Estate as soon as he'd personally thanked tonight's performer for coming and turned everything over to his manager.

He let himself into the silent house, reset the alarm and climbed the stairs. Light spilling from a bedroom in the south hallway caught his attention and sent adrenaline pulsing through his veins.

Was there an intruder in the house or was Lauryn still awake and exploring? Had she walked in on a burglary despite the heavy security of the house? Or had one of the housekeeping staff left a light on? The need to see Lauryn, to reassure himself she was okay, suddenly seemed as necessary as breathing. He pulled his cell phone from its clip, ready to dial 911 if necessary, and crept down the hall toward the master suite to check on Lauryn first.

The bed was empty, the spread smooth and undisturbed.

He retraced his steps. The bathroom was dark and deserted. He flipped on the closet light switch. The dress Lauryn had worn tonight lay draped across the center island. She'd made it home and changed. That meant the light in the guest room was probably her. He snapped his phone back into the holder.

In an attempt to get her into bed, he'd turned up the heat since that evening she'd come apart in his arms, and this morning he'd left the lab results declaring them both disease-free on her dresser. He'd also tucked a box of condoms in each bedside table and slipped a jeweled condom compact into her purse. Nothing subtle about that.

Had he pushed too far too fast?

Had he driven Lauryn out of their suite?

He made his way to the guest bedroom. Both the room and bed were unoccupied. Light and a tapping sound came from the walk-in closet. Odd. He silently crossed the room and looked through the door. Lauryn knelt on the floor, rapping her knuckles against the floorboards and then pressing each end.

"What are you doing?"

She screamed, sprang to her feet and spun to face him. One hand covered her chest. "You scared me."

"What are you doing?" he repeated.

Guilt infused her face. She nibbled her bottom lip and hugged her middle. "I'm...I'm looking for a hidden compartment."

That made no sense. He must have misheard. "What?"

She swept a hand through her hair, looked away and then

her gaze returned to his. "This was my mother—my *birth*-mother's house. I'm looking for her diaries."

That made even less sense. "Lauryn, what in the hell are you talking about? Are you drunk?"

But her eyes were clear and she looked steady on her feet. He hadn't seen her drink anything tonight besides her favorite sparkling water with a twist of lime.

"It's a long story. One I should have told you before now and I'm sorry that I didn't. But I didn't know how." The look she gave him made the hair on his nape rise. He wasn't going to like this—whatever *this* was. "Can we— I need to show you something."

She walked toward him and squeezed past him through the door. He followed her to their bedroom closet where she pulled out her suitcase, lifted a liner out of the bottom and extracted two file folders and a pile of letters bound neatly together with a string. She pushed them toward him.

The return address on the letters was the same as this estate. No name. Just the initials *A. L.*

"After my father died I found out I was his child, but not my mother's. Adrianna Laurence was my birthmother. She met my father when he was stationed in Florida. They had an affair and she became pregnant with me. The letters she wrote to him refer to a hidden compartment in the floor of her bedroom closet where she kept her diary hidden. She wrote, 'Only you, me and my diary know the truth.'

"I'm hoping to find the diary and read about their affair. Not the intimate stuff. Just the part about me. And why she gave me away."

He juggled the thoughts bombarding him. There was no way Lauryn could have moved from California to Florida and coincidentally met and married him—the owner of the house her mother had once inhabited. He shifted the folders

and saw Adrianna Laurence's name on one of the tabs and
his on the other.

"You set me up?"

She winced. "Not exactly."

"How *exactly?*"

She exhaled slowly as if buying time. "I came to Florida
briefly after my father's funeral. I wanted to meet Adrianna,
but she was already dead and she had no living relatives. I
asked around and found out the house had been sold. Almost
no one would talk to me. Those who did swore she'd never
had a child." She tapped the file folder. "This is all I could
find out. It isn't enough."

"You want to claim her estate?" He'd heard crazier
schemes to get money. But he hadn't expected such greed
from Lauryn. Okay, sure, she'd married him for a million
bucks, but he hadn't noticed her going on any wild spending
sprees.

"No. I just want the diary or diaries if there's more than
one. A slew of research hours later I found out you'd bought
the Laurence house, and I knew the only way to get what I
wanted was through you."

A sour taste filled his mouth. His stomach churned. "You
used me."

"I guess you could say that. You have to understand,
Adam, I'd just lost my father. And it felt like I'd lost my
identity, too. The woman I'd called 'mother' for twenty-six
years wasn't my mother. My parents' supposedly perfect
marriage was just a sham. My father married Susan, his
best friend's widow, to give me a mother and to give her
baby a father. Everything I'd believed in had been a lie. I
didn't—and still don't—know what's real and what's
fiction. I need to find out the truth—the real truth, not the
fairytale they fed me."

It was almost too much to comprehend. "You said you were an only child. Was that a lie, too?"

She flinched. "Except for tonight when I told you I wanted to come home and catch up on sleep, I haven't lied to you except by omission. Susan's baby was stillborn. She and my father never had any other children."

"Why play out this charade? Why not just tell me what you wanted?"

"Oh please, this whole story is preposterous. Would you have believed me?"

Probably not.

She must have read his answer on his face. She continued, "When I was researching you I came across Estate's Web site, and I saw the job posting for an accountant. It seemed like fate. I'm a qualified CPA and I wanted to spend some time in Florida. So I sent you my résumé. Both it and references are real and verifiable.

"I thought once you and I got to know each other, once you had a chance to discover I'm not some crackpot, I could explain the situation and make my request. But it didn't work out that way. We saw each other at most two hours a week and that was always with other employees around."

He remembered her stipulation. She'd said she'd marry him, but only if they lived here. "You married me to get into this house."

"The marriage was your idea. You approached me."

True. "But the house is what cinched the deal."

"Yes. That and the chance to meet Helene Ainsley and anyone else who might have known my mother."

Lauryn had hunted him down and she'd lied to him.

Lies by omission were still lies and potentially damaging. Look at the havoc his father's affair had wreaked on his family. On Cassie.

"What would you have done if I hadn't proposed?"

"I was trying to work up my courage to approach you, but I was afraid that if I did and you said no, I'd be at a dead end with nowhere else to turn. My questions would never be answered."

She lifted a hand as if to touch his arm, but he backed out of reach. He couldn't let the chemistry between them cloud his judgment.

"Adam, I'm sorry I didn't tell you sooner. I just… I didn't know how."

Anger, confusion, disappointment and a sense of foolishness for being duped warred within him. He felt betrayed. Used.

He wanted to walk away from Lauryn, but dissolving the marriage after only a week would ruin all of his plans. For the council seat. For a larger stake in Garrison, Inc.

But could he trust Lauryn enough to carry on the pretense?

"Did you fake your physical response to me just to string me along?"

He hadn't noticed her pallor until color swept up her neck and flooded her cheeks, but she didn't look away. "You know I didn't."

Her eyes pleaded for understanding, but he didn't know what to think. What to say. What to do.

"When you find the diaries—if they exist—then what?"

"We go on as agreed. I promised you two years. I won't break my word."

Her eyes were clear and earnest. If she was lying she deserved an Oscar.

He picked up the folders and letters. "We'll discuss this in the morning."

She started after him. "Adam—"

He held up a hand. "Back off. I need space right now."

And then he turned and walked away because he wanted to believe her even when everything in him said he shouldn't. Rationally, he knew her story was ludicrous.

And he'd been burned by lies before.

His father's to cover up the affair. His mother's to hide her drinking.

First he'd read the letters and whatever was in the folders and then he'd talk to Brandon to find out where he stood legally in this disaster.

When he had all the facts he'd have to make the decision.

Keep his wife. Or throw her out on her pretty, lying ass.

Eight

"I'll help you look for the diaries."

Adam's voice startled Lauryn so badly she nearly inhaled her orange juice.

He believed her. The balloon of happiness swelling inside her warned her that this was about more than finding the diaries.

She twisted in her chair to face him. Adam looked like he'd slept as poorly as she had. Dark smudges underlined his eyes. He'd already shaved and dressed in charcoal trousers and a black silk shirt even though he didn't have to leave for hours.

Saturdays at Estate were always busy. Lauryn didn't have to go in. She was part of the Monday to Friday staff, but because of the wedding and honeymoon and time spent training her assistant on the new check-writing software they'd recently implemented, Lauryn had fallen behind on a few tasks and wanted to catch up before the Monday deluge of deliveries hit the club.

"Why would you want to help me?"

"Brandon says you haven't broken our contract. Even if I boot you out I'd have to pay you the full million."

She flinched. "I wouldn't take money for a job I didn't finish. But please, let me look for the diaries before we end this."

"We're not ending this yet. I lost my father recently, too. I know how that skews your thinking. And I know what it's like to have unanswered questions."

She fell a little in love with him in that moment. But she squashed those feelings deep inside. Her relationship with Adam was temporary. She couldn't afford to lose her heart to him. Besides, even if she decided she wanted more from their marriage, she wasn't the kind of woman a guy like him ended up with. She'd have to be blind to miss the difference between her and the other guests at the Ainsleys' party or at the posh restaurants where she and Adam dined.

Class vs. brass—of the military brat variety.

Being polite and demure didn't come naturally to her. It was something she'd labored over every day since her annulment.

He poured himself a cup of coffee but leaned against the counter instead of joining her at the table for brunch. "Your story checks out. I found your father's obit online. Sounds like he was a hell of a guy. Shame about the accident."

Adam had checked up on her. She couldn't blame him. "He went out doing what he loved. Flying. Testing new equipment. And still in uniform. The air force defined him. It's better that he died before he had to face retirement."

"My father was the same. He lived for work." A moment of silence passed as if Adam, too, had become lost in his memories and then he shook his head and focused on Lauryn. "I still need you for my original purpose. I want to win that election."

She set her glass on the table, rose and crossed the room, stopping just inches from him. "I won't let you down, Adam."

She'd do whatever it took to help him become the president of the Business Council, and she'd try to make his brother Parker see what a valuable asset he was ignoring.

Rising on tiptoes, she brushed her lips against his cheek. "Thank you."

His arm hooked her around the waist when she would have withdrawn, keeping their lower halves fused. "For what?"

"For helping me. For believing and trusting me."

"You should have been straight with me, Lauryn."

"I know. I'm sorry."

"Are there any other skeletons in your closet I need to know about?"

She considered telling him about her misspent youth. But her rebellious days were long past and wouldn't affect him. Tommy was on the opposite side of the country—very likely in jail somewhere given his yen to make a quick and not always legal buck. Besides, the annulment meant legally her marriage had never happened. Thanks to her father, the ceremony she couldn't remember had been erased from the record books. The whole debacle was too embarrassing for words. She was ashamed of her past, of her obnoxious teenage behavior, her stupid mistakes and her gullibility. And she was afraid Adam would think less of her because of it.

"No."

"Good." He discarded his mug, speared his fingers through her hair and cupped the back of her head. And then he kissed her.

She didn't care if this embrace was window dressing for the housekeeper. All she cared about was the warmth of his mouth and the strength of his body against hers. She hated to admit she'd come to like and even anticipate these public displays of affection a little too much.

He tasted of cinnamon toothpaste and coffee.

His hands slid down her back to grasp her bottom and pull her flush against his tall frame. Hard, hot muscles bunched beneath her hands as she shaped his forearms, biceps and shoulders. His hair was silky and slightly damp from his recent shower, his jaw warm and smooth and freshly shaven.

Adam lifted his head. His labored breaths matched her own and his intense gaze fastened on hers. "Enough. I can't keep driving myself to the brink of control and backing off. I want you, Lauryn, and I'm tired of playing games."

The roughened sound of his voice made her quiver. He was right. They couldn't go on as they'd been. The tension and teasing were getting out of control.

"I want you, too, Adam."

His nostrils flared and his pupils expanded. "Then we can take the day off and start searching the closets. Or we can go back to bed. Together."

Her stomach somersaulted. She wasn't going to fool herself into believing this meant forever. But she liked and respected Adam. And she was halfway in love with him.

"I've waited months to find those diaries. I think I can wait a few more minutes."

His brows shot up as if she'd insulted him, but fire flared in his eyes. "Minutes? You underestimate me, wife."

A smile tugged her lips. "Prove it."

Adam swept Lauryn into his arms and headed out of the kitchen.

Her heart jolted at the sheer romanticism of the gesture. She locked her arms around his neck and held on but squirmed when he reached the foyer and didn't slow down. "Adam, you can't carry me up the stairs."

"Want to bet?"

They met the housekeeper coming down.

"Martina, hold any calls. The wife and I are not to be disturbed."

"*Si*, Señor Garrison." Smiling, Martina hustled away as if eager to give them privacy.

Adam climbed effortlessly. His breathing had barely altered by the time he reached the landing. He strode down the hall, not stopping until he reached their bedroom where he lowered her legs, clamped a hand around her nape and took her mouth. Ravenously.

Lauryn dragged her fingertips from his shoulders down his chest and over the rapidly thudding heart keeping pace with her own. Right or wrong, she'd made the decision to do this, to unleash the passion she'd kept caged for so long, and now she couldn't get him naked fast enough.

Her fingers clutched his shirt and yanked upward, freeing his shirttails and allowing her access to the hair-spattered six-pack she'd admired from his loft Monday morning. She splayed her hands over the hot skin at his waist and soaked up his heat.

Adam snapped his head back and reached for his cuffs while Lauryn started on the buttons of his shirt, working her way from the bottom up. When his cuffs were loose Adam released the top buttons, meeting her in the middle of his chest. As soon as the last disk slipped free, she shoved the silk off his shoulders, revealing dark whorls over his pectorals and the line of hair leading to the waistband of his pants. She raked her nails down the path.

His muscles contracted and air whistled between his clenched teeth. He caught her hands, kissed each palm and then pressed them to her sides. He pushed off her new designer suit jacket. It piled on the floor at her feet. Her blouse became his next target. Making fast work of the buttons, he sent it after her jacket.

Inhaling deeply, he reared back to take in her lavender lace bra. He lifted his hands and with his pointer fingers traced the thin straps from her shoulders down over the swells of her breasts to the tiny bow in the front. He cupped her briefly and then shoved the straps from her shoulders to her elbows, pinning her upper arms by her sides like a lingerie strait-jacket. Then he folded the fabric cups beneath her flesh, exposing her to his devouring gaze.

Her nipples hardened and her internal muscles clenched in anticipation. She held her breath as he bent his head and then his hot, wet mouth engulfed her, laved her, suckled her. She bit her lip on a moan. He rewarded the sound by cradling and caressing her other breast. Need twisted deep inside her. Spiraling. Tightening. She speared her fingers through his hair and held him close until impatience with her restricted movements became too bothersome to bear.

Lauryn reached behind her back, flicked open her bra and shrugged out of the garment. She needed him naked, needed to touch him. Her fingers found and released his leather belt and then the hook of his trousers. She eased the zipper down, reached inside to stroke him and found flesh. Hard. Hot. Smooth. *Bare* flesh.

Gasping, she jerked back. His pants glided past his narrow hips and down his legs. "You're not wearing underwear."

"Never do." Adam kicked his shoes and pants aside. He whipped off his socks and straightened.

His erection rose thick and long from a dense nest of dark, wiry curls. Her fingers curled involuntarily in expectation of touching him, but he captured her hands, laced his fingers through hers and waltzed her backward until the dais on which the raised bed sat bumped her heels.

His arms encircled her, briefly searing his chest to her breasts and his hard length to her belly. Her lungs emptied in a rush. He unbuttoned and unzipped her skirt, letting it drop to the floor to reveal her high-cut lavender lace panties.

"Nice." His growl made the blasé word sound wicked. He knelt, and, hooking his fingers in the elastic, tugged the panties to her ankles. He leaned forward, pressed his cheek to her triangle of curls and inhaled. "Your scent drives me crazy."

Her knees buckled. Adam scooped her up, carried her to the freshly made bed, ripped back the nubby silk spread and lowered her onto to Egyptian cotton sheets. The fabric was cool against her back in contrast to the hot palms skimming her underwear past her ankles, but leaving high-heeled sandals behind.

He sat back on his haunches and looked his fill. "You're beautiful."

She'd heard those words before. But she could see in Adam's eyes that he meant them. He wasn't spewing empty flattery to get what he wanted. He wanted *her.* Not just sex. Not just a female receptacle. *Her.*

And suddenly she realized this wasn't the tawdry, meaningless sex of her teens or the itch to defy her father and test her womanly wings. This was…more. And that worried her a little because "more" wasn't part of their marriage agreement.

Adam feathered the lightest of touches around her ankles, over her calves and shins, moving closer and closer to her apex, but with teasing detours behind her knees, to the outside of her thighs and then finally, finally where she wanted him.

"*Oooh.*" Her hips jolted off the mattress at the electrifying initial contact of his fingers against her center. He stroked, found her wetness and smoothed it over her sensitized flesh with a slightly roughened fingertip.

It was too much. Not enough. Exactly right.

And then his mouth found hers and his tongue plunged deep in tandem with his fingers doing the same much lower. Her cry of ecstasy filled his mouth. He carried her swiftly toward climax, but let her drift back down short of her goal. He repeated his sensual teasing again and again until, tense and desperate, she writhed beside him.

She clutched his hair, his shoulders, his back, begging with actions rather than words. And then she covered his hand with hers, holding him at her center. "Please. Now."

Adam rocked back. His passion-darkened gaze held hers for countless seconds and then he rolled away. Lauryn wanted to scream in frustration, but then she realized what he was doing.

Protection. How could she have forgotten? Even in her crazy, careless, rebellious past she'd never forgotten protection.

He opened the nightstand drawer, withdrew a condom and returned to her.

She should confront him about his cocky assurance that she'd sleep with him. Maybe later.

She snatched the package from his hand, but then made a few torturous detours of her own. He wanted to make her beg? Well, she could return the favor. She lightly scraped her nails over his chest, abdomen, hips and legs, and finally, his sex. His groan, the jerk of his flesh, the dewy drop of arousal at his tip combined to excite her even more. When she couldn't wait another second, she tore open the wrapper and rolled the condom down his rigid length.

Before she could consider her next move he had her flat

on her back, his thighs between hers, and his erection at her entrance. Adam cupped her bottom, lifted and plunged deep.

The air gushed from her lungs on a cry as he filled her. Adam froze with his jaw rigid and his unblinking gaze locked on hers. "Lauryn?"

"Don't stop. Please don't stop."

"You're so damn tight. Were you—"

"No. But it's been a while. This is…good."

The devilish glint returned to his eyes but didn't completely erase the hint of concern. He gently stroked the back of his knuckles across her cheek. "Only good?"

She pressed her heels into the mattress and arched her hips to take him deeper. Pure hunger wiped the smile from his face.

"Really good. *Great.* Adam. I. Can't. Wait. Please."

She didn't have to repeat her request a third time. He withdrew and thrust again and again, suffusing her with a heat that intensified with each powerful surge. With his hands, mouth and body, touching, tasting, thrusting, he rushed her into the fastest and most consuming orgasm of her life. It ripped through her like a tornado, leaving her weak and clinging, winded and shattered. But he wasn't finished. Adam coaxed her into a second and a third before he joined her, his groan echoing through the bedroom.

And then his weight settled over her, his damp skin fusing to hers. Decimated, she held him close, smoothed his tangled hair, stroked his slick back and tried to catch her breath.

Wow. Her teenage affairs had not prepared her for that.

He pulled away and lay beside her, and a hollow feeling opened in her belly, slowing her racing heart.

She wasn't just a little in love.

She'd fallen totally and completely for Adam Garrison.

A man who defined temporary relationships.

She hadn't broken the vow she'd made to save herself for the love of her life. But she'd chosen a man who couldn't love her back.

"How long?" Adam asked Lauryn.

She paused midtap and twisted on her knees in her corner of the empty closet. "How long what?"

"How long since you've had sex?"

Her breath caught and she bit her lip. Pink stained her cheeks. "About two hours."

He shot her a don't-mess-with-me look. She'd been experienced, a sorceress at driving him out of his mind with desire. But tight. Almost virginal tight. The contradiction had nagged Adam in the hours since they'd torched the sheets and steamed the shower stall and then made love again on the bedroom floor. The rug burn on his knees stung like a bitch. But it was worth it. He hoped Lauryn felt the same about the abrasions on her butt.

Damned rug. He'd throw it out and get something softer.

"Nine years," she finally admitted with obvious reluctance.

His mouth dropped open in shock and then he whistled. "No wonder you were convinced you could hold out." A feeling of smugness swelled his chest and a smile tugged his lips. "But that was before you kissed me."

She rolled her eyes. "Don't let your success go to your head."

"My head's not what you're wearing out, sweetheart."

Sweetheart? He didn't know where the endearment had come from. He never called women by pet names.

He resumed tapping on floorboards, shifted to the next quadrant and started his systematic search again. Five minutes later a board gave beneath his hand. He rapped again and heard a distinctive hollow sound. He pressed the end of the board and the opposite end popped up. "Bingo."

"You found it?" Lauryn scrambled over and watched wide-eyed as Adam pried the six-inch-by-two-foot board out of the back corner to reveal the compartment below.

The crazy story was true. He'd only half believed Lauryn when she'd told him.

A dozen leather-bound books the size of paperback novels rested atop a blue lining—a silk scarf, maybe. There were other items in the space. Envelopes, bound together with a yellowed ribbon. A small, carved wooden box and a few trinkets.

He looked at Lauryn. With her hands clasped in front of her chest, she stared at the booty as if hypnotized but made no move to pick up any of the items.

"You okay?"

She blinked. Looked at him. Inhaled raggedly. "I had almost given up on finding them."

After fruitlessly searching three closets with her today so had he.

"I-I'm a little afraid to read them."

And then he got it. "You're worried you might not like what Adrianna has to say."

"Yes. Does that sound stupid?" Her worried expression snagged something in his chest.

"No. I want to know why my father passed me over, but I'm not sure I would have liked his answer. He wasn't known for pulling his punches."

Sympathy softened her eyes.

Adam reached over the compartment and covered Lauryn's linked hands, sharing a connection he'd never felt with his siblings or any one else. He wasn't the touchy-feely type, and while he'd rather run from the emotional upheaval he expected would follow their discovery, he suspected she might need his support over the next few hours.

"Want privacy?"

"No!" she answered quickly. Too quickly. And then she shook her head and squared her shoulders. "I'm sorry. That was silly. If you'll help me carry all this to the bedroom then you can go to work. You could still get there before Estate opens tonight. I'll be fine. Honest."

He couldn't deny the relief surging through him and yet there was also an odd reluctance to leave her. "You bet."

Using the blue fabric as a catchall, he gathered the corners and then lifted and stood. Lauryn's gasp stopped him. She reached into the hole and picked up one remaining object. A piece of paper.

She scanned the page. "It's my birth certificate. My original one."

The turbulent tangle of emotions in her eyes made him want to do something. He wasn't sure what. Hold her? Surely not. "Let's get this to the bedroom."

He waited while she shakily rose to her feet and then followed her out of the room, down the hall and into their suite where he deposited the stash on the small table set in the bow of the window. He studied her pale face, the birth certificate trembling in her hands and decided to get out before he did something sappy like take her into his arms.

Sex was one thing. Getting emotionally embroiled in her affairs was another. "You're sure you don't need me to stay?"

"No. Saturday's Estate's busiest night. And I—I should probably do this alone."

Vulnerable. That's it. Lauryn looked vulnerable—not an adjective he'd ever attached to her before. She was a lot of things—capable, intelligent, composed, beautiful and sexy as hell—but never vulnerable.

He brushed her cheek with his fingertips. "You have my cell number. Call if you need me."

Adam walked away.

But it wasn't nearly as easy as it should have been.

* * *

"You're still awake," Adam said.

Startled, Lauryn looked at him and then checked the clock. Six in the morning already. She'd read through the night. Eight hours. She closed the diary she'd been rereading for the third time—the one detailing her mother's pregnancy and Lauryn's birth.

"She wanted me." Her voice sounded hoarse from the emotion dammed in her throat. She swiped at her dry and scratchy cried-out eyes.

Adam approached slowly. "You doubted that?"

"Of course I doubted that. She gave me away and never tried to contact me even though she knew exactly where I was." And Lauryn had thought so much worse—that she'd been a baby even a mother couldn't love. "But she kept me for two weeks. She tried to be my mother."

Lauryn tapped the stack of diaries. "I don't understand some of the medical terminology in these, but Adrianna had a heart condition. The doctors and her family told her to abort me because it wasn't safe for her to carry a baby to term. She refused and ran away. No one in Miami knows about me because she never told anyone that she'd had a baby and given it up for adoption. Her family thought she'd gone away to have the abortion."

Searching her face, Adam knelt beside her putting his face on level with hers. "This is good?"

She sensed his wariness. Did he expect her to fall apart all over him? Admittedly she'd had a few rocky moments as she read the diaries and her father's letters to Adrianna, but those were private. She wouldn't inflict that on him.

A smile tickled her lips. "Yes. This is good. I have my answers, the ones I craved, and I have you to thank for that."

"No thanks necessary."

She couldn't help touching him. Cradling his face in her hand, Lauryn dragged her fingertips over the beard stubble shadowing his jaw line. His lips were soft against the pad of her thumb, and despite her roller-coaster night desire tightened her middle.

"Adrianna died at thirty-six. I'm ten years from that age. I needed to know if there were health time bombs in my DNA that my regular physicals hadn't picked up. But what she had wasn't hereditary. She contracted an infection in her early teens that weakened her heart muscle. She claims her parents smothered her from then on, never letting her live like a normal woman.

"And then she met my father in Fort Lauderdale while he was on leave. He was the first man who didn't treat her like she was damaged goods because he didn't know. She fell in love with the dashing air force pilot that week even though she knew they had no future. Besides the class differences, my father had already been reassigned to California and was leaving within the month.

"When she discovered she was pregnant eight weeks later she saw having me as her one chance to do what normal women do and she decided not to have the abortion. But the pregnancy weakened her heart, and she was afraid she wouldn't be strong enough to raise a child *if* she survived the delivery. She contacted my father when she was seven months along." Lauryn's throat closed up. Her mother had risked dying to have her.

"I read what he wrote her, Adam. When my father found out about me he proposed, but Adrianna turned him down. There were hints to that in her letters to him when she said she couldn't do as he asked or that he shouldn't try to turn a vacation romance into something it was never meant to be. But I didn't know he'd proposed.

"He wanted me. When Adrianna realized she wasn't strong enough for shared custody they made the arrangements for the adoption. And my father found the perfect solution in Susan, his best friend's pregnant widow.

"After turning me over to my father Adrianna moved back here and had very little life outside these walls. It's kind of sad." Lauryn's voice broke the last word into two syllables.

Adam rose, pulling her into his arms and holding her tight.

She rested her head over his heart, taking strength from the strong, steady beat. Being with him like this felt right. It was as if she'd found her past and her future right here in this house with him. She tipped back her head and met his gaze and realized she had more than DNA in common with her birthmother.

Like Adrianna, Lauryn had fallen for a man with whom she had no future, and like her birthmother, Lauryn intended to make the most of her time with him.

And then she'd let him go. Even if it ripped out her heart.

Nine

Lauryn smelled coffee and her lagging energy revived.

She turned in her office chair and spotted her husband with a to-go cup in one hand and a bag bearing the same familiar logo in the other and a mischievous glint in his eyes. That glint did crazy things to her pulse.

She held up a finger and pointed to her telephone headset.

Adam entered her office and hitched his hip on the corner of her desk.

Almost every day since she'd started working at Estate she'd ducked out around three to get coffee from a nearby shop, but today her assistant had discovered a discrepancy in a delivery that she hadn't been able to unravel. Lauryn had taken over and was still tied to her desk trying to fix it.

"So you'll deliver the missing items first thing in the morning? We must have them the day after tomorrow for the Thanksgiving Day event." She waited for confirmation and then finished the call. Removing the headset, she smiled at Adam, who extended the cup.

"Thanks." She gratefully sipped the chocolate coffee brew. Perfect. Had he known what she always ordered? Or had the barista told him?

He set the bag on her blotter. "Did you know your favorite coffee shop sells five brands of condoms along with the coffee, protein shakes and croissants?"

"I can't say I ever noticed that." But South Beach shops had their idiosyncrasies, so it didn't surprise her.

"You can ask me to bring you coffee anytime, along with anything else the store sells." He added a wink that made her stomach somersault. If this was the way he charmed his women, then it was no wonder "legions" fell at his feet.

He opened the bag to reveal the contents. "Which is your favorite brand?"

Her body caught fire. "Whichever one you're wearing."

"Good answer, wife." He came behind her desk, cradled her face and stroked a thumb over her lips. Her internal muscles clenched and her toes curled. The sex between them had been amazing, and while she should be sated since she'd left his bed mere hours ago, her hormones seemed to be set on simmer whenever Adam was around.

He never missed an opportunity to touch her. To the employees streaming past her open door as the day shift left and the evening crew arrived, he no doubt looked the picture of a devoted, concerned husband. Sometimes he even fooled her.

"You look like you could use a siesta. Want to go home for a couple of hours before returning tonight?" His velvety tone implied resting wasn't the only thing on the agenda. Her skin tingled in anticipation.

She was tired, but happier than she'd ever been. Since

they'd first made love three days ago Adam had abandoned the sofa bed in the sitting room. Loving him and then falling asleep in his arms was far better than any fantasy she could have dreamed up.

Oh sure, she knew there was a good chance there would be a train wreck around the bend with her name on it, but she'd face losing Adam when—*if*—the time came. In the meantime, she'd try to show him why they should renegotiate the two-year clause in their marriage contract.

She covered his hand on her cheek with hers and turned her lips into his palm.

"Get a room," Ricco, Estate's booking agent, called from the open doorway with a wide grin. The staff surprisingly had accepted the marriage without incident. If there'd been any snide comments, Lauryn hadn't heard them. "Lauryn, I have the estimates you wanted."

Adam shifted his hand to Lauryn's nape, clearly marking his territory the way he did each night at Estate, when they went out to eat or at the Garrison Sunday dinners. She knew the gesture was merely for show, but deep in her heart she wished it were more.

Lauryn took the paper Ricco offered with an unsteady hand. When—*if*—her marriage to Adam ended she'd have to leave Estate, and she dreaded that. She liked her coworkers, liked her job and even liked South Beach's quirky atmosphere, but there was no way she could survive hearing the rumors about Adam's latest conquests or seeing the pictures in the gossip columns—pictures that now featured her.

The media blitz Adam had predicted before they'd married had hit. Lauryn braced herself each morning before she opened the paper. She'd found her own face in the society pages several times in the past twelve days since Brandon had issued the press release.

Adam stood. "She'll have to get back to you on those tomorrow, Ricco. We're heading out for a few hours, but we'll be back tonight before the doors open."

His dictatorial tone allowed no room for comment. Funny, but Lauryn's hackles didn't even twitch even though she had a mountain of work waiting on her desk.

"Not a problem." Ricco waved and left them.

Adam extended his hand. "Let's go home, wife."

She grabbed her purse and accompanied Adam outside. He helped her into his car and then scanned the grounds surrounding the club before turning back to her. "The barista said a guy was asking for you at the coffee shop today. Any clue who that might be?"

Her heart jolted, but she dismissed the momentary alarm. "It's probably just another reporter."

Who else could it be?

"You've become a creature of habit, babe."

The voice from her past brought Lauryn to a dead stop as she approached the coffee shop counter. Her stomach pitched. She spun toward the man lowering the newspaper that had been hiding his face.

Tommy.

Ice crackled through her veins.

He sat by a window with a clear view of Estate's employee entrance. Her ex still looked like a biker bad boy from his long brown hair to his Fu Manchu beard and ragged jeans. He tilted back in his chair with a sneer on his face that she'd once found fascinating. Not anymore.

Why had she ever found him attractive?

Because everything about him from his tattoos to his ponytail made your father crazy.

She'd been an idiot to think rebelling would win her

parents' respect, and convincing herself she'd been in love with Tommy had been the height of stupidity.

"Never expected you to turn out so much like your old man. How is the Sergeant?"

"Dead," she replied coldly. "Why are you here?"

"'Cuz we have unfinished business."

"Wrong. What we had was over a long time ago—the day you asked me to be your drug mule," Lauryn whispered and glanced at the curious barista three yards away who stood goggle-eyed with Lauryn's drink already prepared in her hand. She hoped Jan hadn't overheard.

"Thanks, Jan." Lauryn quickly paid for the beverage and then she turned and left the coffee shop without looking back. Whatever Tommy wanted he wouldn't leave until he got it. She heard his boots on the sidewalk behind her as she quickly walked a couple of blocks without stopping until she reached the Ocean Drive beachfront park. She hoped there were no reporters in the vicinity.

"What? You don't want to talk in front of your friends?"

She pitched the drink in a trash can. There was no way she could put anything in her stomach and keep it down. She glared at Tommy. "What do you want?"

His brown eyes raked Lauryn from head to toe. "I see you've married yourself a millionaire. The expensive duds look good on you. A little boring, but not too bad."

She folded her arms and said nothing.

"Too bad that marriage ain't legit."

How could he know about her marriage contract with Adam? "What are you talking about?"

"Our annulment wasn't legal."

Her heart slammed against her ribs and her stomach dropped to her sandals. "Of course it was."

"That means your marriage to moneybags isn't, either."

He tapped the breast pocket of his leather jacket. "Got proof the annulment wasn't signed, sealed and delivered. Your daddy forgot to dot all his i's and cross all his t's."

"He didn't forget." *He wouldn't. He couldn't.* Her father was—had been—anal to the core. He'd never slip up on something as important as separating his daughter from the man he called a thug. Turns out he'd been right about Tommy.

"You sure about that, babe? Because I'm willing to show what I got to the press. They think you're so goddamned perfect. But they don't know you like I do. Bet that new husband of yours doesn't, either."

Panic seized her. She fought to conceal it. Tommy, she'd learned the hard way, fed on out-of-control emotions. In fact, hindsight told her he'd often incited them—the way he had when he'd convinced her she deserved to go to Tijuana for spring break.

"You're bluffing."

"You willing to gamble on that?"

Lauryn's father had handled everything from the moment he'd picked her up in Mexico. She'd been eighteen, scared out of her mind and more than willing to let Rodney Lowes take control. The only part Lauryn had played was to pee in a cup for a drug test and sign where he'd told her on the annulment petition. There'd been a seemingly endless pile of documents.

All she had to do was get her copy of the annulment decree from her father's papers. But his papers were in a safety-deposit box in California, and her mother, the one with the key to that box, was away on a cruise until Tuesday. Susan couldn't retrieve and fax what Lauryn needed.

"Let me see your proof."

He pulled out what looked like an official document, but held it out of reach. "Uh, uh, uh. No touching. I'm not having you run off with it."

"What's wrong with it? It looks fine."

"Besides the missing official raised seal that means the clerk or notary or whoever never sealed the deal? There's this." He shifted his thumb to reveal a faded red "DENIED" stamp.

Her world stopped. Could the officials refuse to grant an annulment? Her father would have told her. He would have helped her get a divorce. Wouldn't he?

"We're still married, babe."

Tommy had to be scamming her. *He had to be.* But she had no way of proving him wrong right here, right now. Even if she could get her mother to call the bank and authorize them to open the safety-deposit box for Lauryn, tomorrow was Thanksgiving Day. Getting a last-minute flight to California would be impossible, and she couldn't exactly request the Garrison's corporate jet service or ask Adam to fly her if she wanted to keep Tommy's threat and her shameful past a secret.

"You know this is bullshit, Tommy. What do you want?" She fought a grimace at her choice of words. *Trashy mouth. Trashy morals.* How many times had her father said those words during her teens? Back then he'd been right and she'd cursed just because she knew how much he hated to hear a woman swear.

Apparently Tommy had resurrected one of her bad habits.

Tommy rocked back on his booted heels and slipped the papers back into his inside jacket pocket. "A little green could make this go away."

"That's extortion."

"I call it insuring your future happiness."

She scanned the park. As usual there were uniformed police officers within shouting distance. "I could call one of those cops over here and report you."

"Go for it. But then the paper would get wind of your bigamist marriage."

Her knees weakened. *Bigamy.* True or untrue, even a hint of this would destroy Adam's credibility and his bid for the council nomination. She cared too much about him to let that happen. And cared too much for him to let him find out what a selfish, irresponsible imbecile she'd once been.

He'd said more than once that he wanted a conservative, proper wife. And she'd been about as far from that as you could get. Telling him the truth meant losing his respect and any chance of convincing him to try to make this marriage permanent.

He'd despise her. Maybe as much as she despised herself.

And then a niggling doubt made Lauryn's back itch. She couldn't remember ever seeing the final annulment decree.

Maybe Tommy wasn't bluffing.

Resignation settled on her shoulders as heavily as Atlas's globe.

She needed time. Time to prove Tommy's accusations were untrue. And she'd have to buy it. "I don't have a lot of cash."

"C'mon, babe, he's a Garrison. One of Miami's most eligible bachelors according to the Internet."

"Former bachelors."

He dipped his head to indicate his pocket. "Is he?"

Despite Adam's plan to pay for Lauryn's makeover, Lauryn had used her own money for the clothes, makeup and hairdresser believing it would give her the freedom to back out of the marriage right up until the last minute if she wanted. All she had liquid was the first monthly marriage payment.

"What'll it take to shut you up? Five thousand?"

"Babe, I wasn't born yesterday. Give me a hundred grand."

"I don't have a hundred thousand dollars!"

"Your husband does."

"Our accounts are separate. I can't touch Adam's money."

"Then I'm talking to the papers." He turned as if to walk away.

Lauryn grabbed his arm. She couldn't let him go, couldn't let him destroy Adam's plans. "Tommy, I'm not lying. I don't have that kind of money and I can't get it."

"Then how much you got?"

If she low-balled him he'd walk. But it galled her to have to reward his evil streak. "Twenty-five thousand."

"Not good enough." He tried to shake her free, but she dug her nails deeper into his biceps.

She couldn't believe this was happening. "I can get my hands on forty thousand dollars. That's it. I swear it."

His eyes narrowed as he appraised her, and he must have seen the truth on her face. "Let's take a walk to your bank. But remember, babe, one peep out of you and I go to the press."

"Lauryn, you okay?" Adam called out as Lauryn passed his open office door.

"Yes," she replied quickly—too quickly—and kept walking. *Tell him.*

But she couldn't. Not yet. Not until she fixed this disaster. She dumped her purse in her desk drawer and pressed cold fingers to her temples.

"You were gone longer than usual," Adam said behind her, startling her into whipping around and lowering her hands.

"I…had a…headache and I took a walk on the beach to get rid of it." She was lying. Sort of. Tommy was a headache and she had taken a walk to get rid of him. But she hated twisting the truth.

"You're pale." With concern in his eyes Adam crossed the room, cupped her shoulders and examined her face. "Need to go home?"

She needed to wash off the stench of Tommy and to come up with a plan. How could she get copies of the documentation she needed? She didn't even know the name of the attorney her father had used back then. Susan would know, but her mother would be gone six more days. Was there a way to call her onboard the ship? But even if she did get a name most offices, public and private, would be closed for the holidays until Monday.

Lauryn's chest tightened. She could lose Adam over this. And she wasn't ready to let him go yet. Who was she kidding? She'd never be ready to end this marriage.

"Lauryn?"

"Hold me. Just hold me." She wound her arms around his waist and pressed her cheek to his shoulder over the steady thump of his heart.

Adam shifted. She heard the click of her office door closing, and then his arms banded around her. His lips brushed her hair.

She lifted her head, chasing his mouth until her lips covered his. His hands tightened on her waist, but he didn't push her away. His mouth opened over hers, his tongue seeking and stroking hers. Lauryn kissed him back with every ounce of love she had in her, and for a moment he almost made her forget the disaster her life had become, the disaster she could make of his.

She shaped him with her hands, memorizing the curve of his skull, the sharp angles of his jaw and the breadth of his shoulders. Her palms flattened over the muscles of his back, his waist, his tight behind. Adam sucked in a sharp breath.

She drew back and looked into his eyes, the eyes of the

man she loved. The man she would lose if she couldn't make this right. "If we don't stop we're going to violate part of the employee handbook."

His nostrils flared and his eyes flashed. Streaks of arousal darkened his cheekbones. "Who are they going to complain to? I'm the boss. Where's your purse?"

"My desk drawer. Why?"

"Because I'm too old to carry condoms in my wallet."

"I don't have any, either."

"Give me your bag."

Alarm shot through her. Her copy of the bank withdrawal slip was in her purse. "Why?"

"I put a condom compact in there last week."

She'd never heard of a condom compact, but it didn't take a genius IQ to figure out what one was. "I'll get it."

While she retrieved her bag and searched inside, Adam locked the office door.

Her fingers closed around a metal square she hadn't noticed before today, but then she rarely had to go into her purse. Adam paid for everything and her keys, lipstick and cell phone went in an outside pocket. The brushed gold lid had her initials engraved on it. *LLG*. Lauryn Lowes Garrison.

Her heart hitched. How long would she bear that name?

She pushed the button and the top opened to reveal a cellophane packet. "What will they think of next?"

"Come here, wife." He took her purse and the compact, dropping the first back into the drawer and the second on the desktop. "Remind me to buy a sofa for your office."

And then he yanked her close and kissed her. Lauryn soaked up his barely leashed desire and reveled in his hurried caresses. His heat, his scent, his taste, she stored them all away in her memory bank. Just in case.

She'd have to tell him about Tommy and when she did

Adam would probably hate her. He'd asked her if she had any more skeletons in her closet and she'd said no. He'd never believe she'd honestly thought her past a nonissue. How naive of her.

But she wanted to get through Thanksgiving dinner at his mother's first and maybe even his mother's birthday party, which Adam was hosting at the club. And then she'd tell Adam the whole sordid truth and pray he understood. Pray he wouldn't hold her youthful indiscretions against her. Pray he wouldn't throw her out.

Adam's mouth traced the cords of her neck while his hands found the zip of her dress. She tore at the buttons of his shirt, his belt, his pants. He had them both naked in seconds. His hot flesh burned her palms, her lips, her tongue. She couldn't get enough of him. She dropped to her knees and took him into her mouth.

"Lauryn," he groaned and speared his fingers her hair. Far too soon he tugged her to her feet and kissed her hard. "I love what you do to me, but right now I need to be inside you."

He backed her toward her wooden two-drawer lateral file cabinet, lifted her onto the cool surface and stepped between her legs. With movements as frantic as hers, his hands shaped her breasts, tweaked her nipples, found her center.

Conscious of employees on the other side of the door, Lauryn shoved a knuckle into her mouth to stifle a cry. She curled the fingers of her other hand around him and stroked his erection. Adam's muffled groan vibrated against her breast, increasing the heavy desire boiling like lava in her center.

He straightened, hooked his hands beneath her knees and pulled her toward him. As soon as she'd rolled on the condom she guided him home and gasped as he filled her. Again and again, he thrust hard and fast.

His hands on her breast and where their bodies joined rushed her toward completion. *Too soon. Too soon. Wait.* She wanted to make it last, to savor the rising heat and the building tension, but climax broke over her like a bursting levy, and she couldn't hold back the waves of ecstasy roaring through her.

His mouth swallowed her cries, and then he fed them back to her as his own orgasm shuddered through him. His head fell to her shoulder. The sound of their labored breathing filled the room and his back heaved beneath her hands.

Her eyes stung. She pulled him closer until not even a piece of paper could slip between their sweat-dampened torsos.

A sense of loss welled within her. She couldn't give this up. Couldn't lose him.

And she'd be damned if she'd let Tommy Saunders ruin this for her without a fight.

Ten

"I want more money."

Tommy.

Lauryn nearly dropped the bedroom phone. She turned and saw Adam just yards away in the bathroom shaving in preparation for Thanksgiving dinner with his family.

"I don't have more," she whispered.

"Don't mess with me, Lauryn. I'm looking at your digs right now. If you don't believe me look out the back window. The place is worth millions."

She walked to the window, looked out at the canal and spotted a small fishing boat with Tommy at the helm. A wave of dizziness reminded her to inhale. "I can't get more."

"Hock something."

"No."

"Then give me that rock on your finger. Tell moneybags

you lost it. He'll buy you another one. Hell, the ring's probably insured. He won't even miss the dough."

She glanced at her engagement and wedding rings and curled her fingers into a fist. She may have come into the rings in an unorthodox manner, but she wasn't giving them up. She checked the bathroom and found Adam scraping away the last of the white foam. "I can't do that."

"Then this canary is gonna sing."

"Don't. Please. Give me a few days. A week." By next Tuesday her mother would be home and Lauryn could fly to California and get the paperwork she needed. She wasn't about to give Tommy more money. Because she realized now he'd just keep coming back.

"You say something, sweetheart?" Adam said from the other side of the bedroom.

"Don't call again," she said into the phone and hung up. "It was someone wanting a donation."

Another twisted version of the truth.

There's a price for every lie you tell. Before you open your mouth, be sure you're prepared to pay it.

She faced Adam. He strolled toward her with his chest bare above his trousers, his face smooth and his eyes searching hers. She couldn't believe how much she loved him. She'd never felt anything even remotely close to this for Tommy.

"Ready for another meal with the Garrisons?"

She didn't think she could eat again until the Tommy issue was resolved. "Can't wait."

"Liar."

The blood drained from Lauryn' head with dizzying swiftness. He had no idea how right he was.

"You've survived two Sunday dinners. You can handle

today." Adam pulled her into his arms and nuzzled a kiss below her ear. "Next year we'll have everybody over here."

She prayed there would be a next year, but at the rate she was going that seemed unlikely.

The ring of his cell phone jarred Adam out of a deep sleep Friday morning.

He forced open a leaded eyelid and looked at the clock. Eight. He'd only been home two hours and the sheets had barely had time to cool after he'd made love to Lauryn. She stirred beside him. He kissed her temple. "Go back to sleep. I got it."

The phone bleated again. Adam slid out of bed and stumbled to the dresser. He snatched up the cell phone and started toward the study so as not to disturb Lauryn as he punched the Receive button. His eyes were too bleary to read the caller ID. "Adam Garrison."

"Have you seen the paper?"

Parker.

"No. I was asleep. We had a big bash at Estate last night. You know I keep vampire hours."

"Your wife made the front page."

Adam's steps stalled in the hall. He turned back to stare at the curvy mound in the bed. "Lauryn? Why?"

"Her husband is claiming she's a bigamist."

"I did no such—"

"Not you. Her *first* husband."

A DEA raid would have been less shocking. "Her first husband? Lauryn's never been married."

The woman in question bolted upright with her eyes wide and something in their depths that soured Adam's stomach.

"That's not what this guy says," Parker continued. "What's more, he's claiming she's a tramp who stayed just this side of the law. You're in deep shit, little brother. I've already put a call in to Brandon for you. You'd better ask your wife who the hell Tommy Saunders is and if she's still married to him."

The dial tone sounded.

Adam lowered the phone and stared at Lauryn. Her face was as pale as the white sheets. "Who is Tommy Saunders?"

She closed her eyes and swallowed. A pained expression crossed her features. "My ex-husband."

"You said you'd never been married."

"I haven't. Technically." She clutched the sheet to her collarbones, reminding Adam of his own nakedness.

The burn of betrayal lit his skin. He yanked on his robe. "Explain *technically*."

"I ran away with Tommy soon after I turned eighteen. To Tijuana. For spring break. He asked me to marry him. I said no, but I woke up married. He'd drugged me. I don't even remember the ceremony. And then he told me he wanted to make us rich by using me as his drug mule to ferry cocaine out of Mexico. I freaked and ran and called my father. Daddy came and got me, and he handled the annulment." The words poured from her in a rush, but the meaning was clear.

"You were married."

"No. An annulment means the marriage is erased. Like it never happened."

"But it did happen."

"Yes, but—"

"You lied. *Again.*" Something inside him curled up and died.

"Adam, please—"

"How many other lies are there, Lauryn? How many more ways do you plan to screw me?"

"I didn't think my past mattered."

"According to Parker, it's front-page news. I told you I needed a conservative wife."

"And that's what you got. I'm not the selfish girl I was back then."

"No. Now you're the woman that girl turned into. One who set up, used and lied to her husband. If we're even legally married." He shoved a hand through his hair. "Are we?"

She bit her lip. "I think so."

Damnation. "What the hell does that mean?"

"Tommy claims our annulment never went through. I think he's lying. I paid him to be quiet—"

"You paid him? Paid him how much?"

She curled her knees into her chest. "He asked for money and threatened to go to the press if I didn't pay him. I gave him forty thousand dollars to keep quiet until I could find the paperwork and prove he was lying. But then he wanted more and I couldn't give it to him."

"That's who called yesterday?"

Her hesitation nearly crippled him. "Yes."

Another lie.

She climbed from the bed. The sight of her naked body hit him low and hard before she dragged on the robe she'd left draped across the end of the bed two hours ago. How could he still want her when he knew she was a liar?

"My father was detail-oriented in the extreme and a control freak. I know he wouldn't be sloppy like Tommy claims. If the annulment was denied Daddy would have pushed for a divorce. But I never had a copy of the annulment, so I can't prove Tommy's lying. Not yet. My father's papers are locked in a safety-deposit box in Sacramento, and my mother is away on a cruise. I'll fly to Sacramento and as soon as she gets home and I'll get a copy of all the documentation."

She'd ripped his guts out. Personally. Professionally.

"Adam. Please. Let me explain."

"I think you've said more than enough."

"I love you," she whispered.

Another lie. But this one hurt worse than all the rest combined.

Because he loved her.

He'd fallen in love with his beautiful, lying wife.

And right now he couldn't stand the sight of her. Adam stormed into the closet, yanked down his suitcase and started throwing clothes into it.

"What are you doing?" she whispered.

"Getting away from you. I'm moving back to the condo."

"I'll make it right. I'll fix it. Please just give me a chance. All I need is time."

"You've run out of chances with me, Lauryn. Save it for the next sucker."

She silently watched him dress. A lone tear streaked down her cheek before she dashed it aside.

He returned to the bedroom and thrust a pen and pad of paper at her. "Write down everything you know about your boyfriend. His name. A physical description. Where he's staying. I'm having him arrested for extortion."

She hesitated. And that brief moment combined with the regret and worry in her eyes shattered what was left of his battered heart. She must still have feelings for the jerk.

And then something bitter and ugly coiled inside him.

How blind can you be, Garrison?

"Did you call your lover the minute I proposed and cook up this scheme to get more cash?"

"No. And Tommy isn't my lover. He hasn't been for nine years."

"Forgive me for having a little trouble believing you." He slammed the suitcase closed. "You and the bastard deserve each other."

"Adam, you're wrong."

"Forget your big plans. You won't get another dime out of me, *sweetheart*."

She flinched at his acidic endearment.

He grabbed his suitcase and his keys and headed for the front door. When he reached the bottom of the stairs he couldn't help but look back.

Lauryn stood on the landing, both hands clutching her robe. "Adam, I'm sorry. I never meant for you to get hurt."

"Sorry? You're *sorry?* Lauryn, you have destroyed everything, *everything* that matters to me. Sorry doesn't cut it."

He turned on his heel, went out the front door and slammed it behind him.

Paparazzi milled on the other side of the wrought iron gate, circling like vultures around the corpse of his marriage.

"I don't want any more surprises," Adam said to Brandon. "I want to know every single detail Lauryn neglected to mention."

"Then you need a good private investigator. Ace Martin is the guy for the job. He's discreet and fast." Brandon pulled a business card from his wallet.

Adam knocked back his bourbon. "Hell, for all I know Lauryn could be the Jefferies brothers' spy."

Brandon's head jerked up and his eyes sharpened. "Is that likely?"

As the Garrison, Inc. lawyer Brandon knew about the troubles the company had been having with info being leaked. "I don't know. Maybe. She keeps to herself. She has access to a lot of confidential financial information, but more from Estate than Garrison, Inc. I'll ask your P.I. friend to look into it."

"Do you think she's involved?"

"I hope not." Because if she was Garrison, Inc. would have to prosecute, and while he was furious, and yes, hurt, dammit, he didn't want to send her to jail.

Brandon extended the business card to Adam.

Adam rose from the sofa and crossed the library to take it, but at the last second Brandon snatched it out of reach. "You fell for her."

Adam recoiled. "Wrong."

"You did. You fell for Lauryn Lowes. Even Cassie saw and commented on the sparks between you."

"That was lust." He'd never lied to Brandon before, but Adam refused to admit Lauryn had completely duped him. Hooked him. Duped him. And given him the best sex of his life.

"You've been lied to by women before, and it's never bothered you this much."

Adam crossed to the drinks tray and helped himself. He was as at home in Brandon's place as Brandon was in his. In fact, he was more comfortable at Brandon's than at his brothers'.

"I'm not bothered. I'm pissed off. Everything I've been working toward has been destroyed. Bigamy, for godsakes."

"She would be the one guilty of a crime *if* her ex is telling the truth. Not you."

"I hope to hell he's not. And you're wrong. I haven't been screwed over like this before."

"That's your third drink. One of the things I respect about you, Adam, is that you're around liquor all the time, but you don't abuse it. Are you planning to change that tonight?"

Adam splashed a finger of Booker's into his glass. "I'll take a cab home. You won't be sued for negligence for letting me drink and drive."

"That's not what worries me. And you have been screwed over. What about that redhead who was secretly having an affair with Parker and you at the same time? Or the brunette who faked a pregnancy to try to get a wedding ring out of you. Or—"

Adam winced and held up a hand. "You've made your point. But I wasn't in love with any of them."

Brandon noted Adam's slip by cocking his head.

Damn. Adam emptied his glass. The liquor burned all the way down his throat and hit his stomach like acid. He wanted to drink himself into oblivion. To forget Lauryn Lowes and her lover. His marriage. His decimated plans to win more say in Garrison, Inc.

Parker would never take him seriously now.

But drowning his sorrows ran a little too close to his mother's problem.

"At least Cassie's honest," he muttered under his breath.

"Cassie and I think Lauryn is, too." Brandon refilled his own tumbler. "Lauryn's right. In the eyes of the law once a marriage is annulled no valid marriage ever existed, and the grounds for getting a legal annulment aren't easy to get around. Maybe you'd better focus on that."

Adam looked at Brandon in surprise. His best friend would not mislead him. Intentionally. "You're saying her 'he drugged me and married me' excuse could be the truth?"

"Absence of consent is a valid reason for annulment, but she would have had to prove it. Let Ace find out the details for you. He can also check into her other questionable stories."

"The stuff about her birthmother sounds preposterous, but

it's true. I told you about the letters, diaries and the birth certificate."

"So you did. And you're sure Lauryn doesn't want to petition the Laurence estate? If she wanted money approaching the executers should have been her first move. From what you said she found in that compartment, confirmation of her identity and even a DNA match is a real possibility."

Adam rubbed the back of his neck. Brandon had a point. The Laurence estate was worth far more than the million Lauryn had planned to get out of him. And *he'd* approached *her* about the marriage and the money. Not the other way around.

Could he be wrong about her? Was she telling the truth? Or had she and Saunders concocted a scheme to bleed Adam dry?

And did it matter? Hell yes.

Was she still in love with Saunders? Was she still married to the bastard?

Adam couldn't think about that now when he had enough bourbon in his system to make him want to put his fist through something. Or someone. Saunders.

He caught Brandon subtly checking his watch and realized how late it was. "Why aren't you with Cassie tonight?"

"Because you needed me."

"Yeah. Thanks."

"Are you okay with me marrying your half sister?"

"Brandon, I'm closer to you than I am to my own brothers. As far as I'm concerned, making you an official part of my family is just a formality." He offered his hand and then yanked Brandon close in a bump-shoulders-slap-on-the-back embrace. "I owe Cassie for letting me borrow you tonight."

"She'll join me tomorrow if she can get away from the hotel or I'll join her."

"Sounds like you're doing a lot of commuting."

"I am, and you need to know that because of that I've decided to open an office in Nassau. There's no point in getting married if I'm never going to see my wife."

"You're closing down here?"

"No. Just adding another branch of Washington & Associates."

"Good. Because I'll need you to handle my divorce."

"Why would you come forward when all the rest of the Garrisons are saying is, 'No comment'?"

"Because you've made a terrible mistake," Lauryn said across the reporter's cluttered desk Saturday afternoon. "Adam is completely innocent in this situation."

She'd decided a counterattack was the only way to end the vicious scandal that Tommy's story had launched, and as much as she hated being the center of attention these days, if pouring out her past for public consumption would clear Adam, then Lauryn would willingly humiliate herself by doing so. She also hoped sending the press on the trail of the missing documentation would cut through the Thanksgiving weekend barriers keeping her from getting to California and the truth.

The reporters had been relentless over the past twenty-four hours. The tabloid press in particular had followed her everywhere, and she'd used that to her advantage—she hoped. First thing this morning she'd gone to the police department, trailed by an assortment of paparazzi, and filed an official report on the extortion.

Adam may have already filed a complaint like he'd said he would, but this was her mistake and she would take the steps to rectify it. The money she'd paid Tommy wasn't hers. She hadn't earned it. It belonged to Adam and she wanted to return it. Maybe then he'd believe she wasn't trying to fleece him.

After leaving the police department she'd called the reporter who'd broken the original story, offered her an exclusive and set a time for this meeting. Lauryn had told the woman the whole sordid story. The only detail she'd held back was the marriage of convenience part.

"Do you believe what you've told me exonerates Adam Garrison?" the reporter asked.

"Yes. He hasn't done anything wrong. The mistakes were all mine. Adam didn't know about my past or my annulment. I honestly believed it wasn't relevant, and I was too ashamed of my rebellious teenage behavior to tell him. I'm not that person anymore and I haven't been for a long time.

"But whether Tommy's claim that our annulment is invalid is true or not, I underestimated his desire to make a fast and easy buck. I paid him to keep quiet because I love my husband and I didn't want to see Adam hurt. But now because of *my* mistakes the best candidate for the presidency of the Miami Business Council is being trashed in the news."

The reporter's gaze sharpened. "So you're officially announcing Adam Garrison's interest in the position?"

"Adam would be a great council president. He knows business and he knows the community. But only he can announce his candidacy. My purpose in coming forward is to make sure you understand he is a victim, not a perpetrator." She gathered her purse and stood. "Will this run in tomorrow's paper?"

"As soon as I've verified a few facts."

The woman's condescending attitude throughout the interview had rubbed Lauryn the wrong way. Her last remark raised Lauryn's hackles. *All right. Gloves off.*

"You should have verified the facts before running the first story. Have you considered what will happen if Tommy Saunders is lying about the annulment being denied and you've falsely accused a Garrison of bigamy? That could be considered libel and your job and credibility would be in jeopardy."

The woman paled, her indolent posture turned stiff and her mouth fell open.

Lauryn turned on her heel and left. She didn't believe for one moment that the Garrisons would go to battle to clear *her* name, but they would to clear Adam's.

Despite the tensions within the family, there was a bond in the Garrison clan that she envied. And maybe sacrificing her pride and her reputation would make Parker step forward and show Adam just how important a part of the family he was.

"What is this?"

Lauryn's heart stuttered Monday afternoon at the anger in Adam's voice. She swiveled in her office chair. He stood in her doorway holding up a copy of Sunday's newspaper folded to display her interview with the reporter.

Drinking in every inch of him from his overlong hair to his collarless black shirt and crisply pressed black trousers, she rose, rounded her desk and closed the door. She stopped just inches from him, and tilted her head back to meet his gaze.

She'd missed him over the past three days and hadn't expected to see him today since Estate was closed. He looked stressed and his blue eyes were hard and unforgiving. Her hopes sank. She'd bared her soul for that interview, hoping he'd read it and understand her choices. Would he ever forgive her for keeping her secrets? Apparently not.

What had his family thought of the article? She hadn't been invited to the Garrison Sunday dinner yesterday, so she didn't know.

"It's me trying to make this right. Until I can get to California and find my copy of the original documents it's the best I can do. I need a couple of days off. My flight leaves at five tomorrow morning. I should return Wednesday evening."

His jaw shifted. "I don't want your help. I'll handle it. In fact, you can stay in California. I'll have your belongings shipped to you along with the divorce papers—if they're necessary."

She nearly staggered from the verbal blow, but she held her ground because this was one fight she couldn't afford to lose. "You're sounding a lot like your 'control freak' brother at the moment."

He scowled.

"Adam, you told me you were trying to live down a past you weren't proud of. Why is it different when it's me?"

"I didn't lie about mine."

"I didn't lie about mine, either. I just didn't tell you things that I thought were irrelevant and that you wouldn't want to hear.

He snorted in disgust. "You're saying you were protecting me?"

"I thought I was, but I guess I was only protecting myself. Remember that conversation we had about birth order affecting personalities? I said only children either rebelled or conformed. You're the one who guessed I'd conformed and before I could correct you, you followed up that statement by saying a wife with a rebellious past was the last thing you needed. But that was exactly what you had and it was too late to change that. I didn't say anything then because I didn't want you to think less of me.

"I wasn't a good kid, Adam. For five years I gave my parents hell. I used to dress and act like a tramp because it garnered the kind of attention that drove my control freak father nuts. I didn't value myself or those who loved me. I'm not proud of that, but I can't change who I was. I can only make sure the person I am now makes the right decisions for the right reasons.

"And the person I am now promised to help you win the council nomination. I'm trying by making sure the public knows the responsibility for this disaster with Tommy was my fault and only my fault. You're totally blameless."

His face stayed hard, expressionless. Was she getting through to him at all?

"So tell me, Adam, what would a man who loved someone enough to elope do in this situation? Would he run at the first obstacle? Because when we expose Tommy's lie—and I'm confident we will—the paper's going to want to know why you married me in the first place if you quit loving me after barely two weeks and at the first obstacle. Talk about making you look capricious to your business council peers. And then your pretense of marrying for the sake of the nomination is going to come to light."

He stiffened. "Is that a threat?"

She sighed. "No. I would never intentionally do anything to hurt you."

"You're the one who should be worried about lies coming to light. The 'crush-at-first-sight' bull you fed the reporter is absurd."

Embarrassment warmed her skin, but she'd promised to be one hundred percent honest with him from now on. No more secrets.

"It's the truth. I was attracted to you from our first inter-view. The attraction only increased after I took the job. You're smart. You have a way with people that makes everyone around you feel at ease and an enthusiasm for your job that's contag-ious. Your employees fall all over themselves to please you— even me.

"But then I heard the rumors about your legions of women and your meaningless affairs and I told myself to get over you. You were living the life I'd left behind—one I never wanted to return to. Only I didn't get over you. I couldn't."

She'd told him before, but he'd blown her off. She needed to say it again, to watch his face when she said the words.

She took a bracing breath. "I love you, Adam. I fell in love with you the day you offered to spend hours on your hands and knees helping me search those walk-in closets, helping me find out about my family because family is important to you. It is to me, too."

Disbelief flickered in his eyes and then he abruptly turned away, dismissing her. "I'm hosting my mother's birthday party here Wednesday night. I don't want you there."

The stab of pain caught her unawares. "We need to present a united front if you want to come out of this with any credibility at all."

He rounded on her. "Don't you get it? Any chance for the nomination or for Parker to take me seriously is gone. Wiped out by your lies."

"I think you're wrong. And I intend to prove it."

Eleven

"Are you sure you're up for this?" Lauryn asked Susan as the cab pulled away from Miami International Airport and headed toward Estate Wednesday night.

"Of course I want to meet your husband and your in-laws. If Adam's an unforgiving sort, then he doesn't deserve you, and I intend to tell him so." Ever the optimist, her mother smiled and squeezed Lauryn's hand. "But I'm sure that won't be necessary. Besides, I've never crashed a party. It might be fun."

The thought of her very proper mother going anywhere without an invitation made Lauryn smile.

She didn't know how she could have forgotten that Susan Lowes had always been her champion. From the moment Lauryn had greeted her mother's ship through the convoluted confession of the diary search, her marriage, Tommy's reappearance and the scandal that had rocked Miami's elite community, Susan had been nothing but supportive. The only question she'd asked was, "Do you love him?"

When Lauryn had answered in the affirmative, Susan had said then they'd better get back Miami and fix this.

No mother, real or adoptive, could be better.

"Thanks for coming. After the way I acted…" Tears burned Lauryn's eyes and choked off her words. "I don't deserve your support."

Susan's fingers tightened. "You were hurt, Lauryn. I understood. I should have insisted your father tell you the truth on your eighteenth birthday the way we'd planned, but with Adrianna already dead—"

"And my rotten behavior…"

"Well, yes, I admit we did take that into consideration. We didn't want to exacerbate the situation. But still, you had the right to know. And then you were so upset after that business with Tommy, we just didn't want to add to your worries."

"I can't apologize enough for my behavior back then. Every rule seemed to hit a hot button and I overreacted."

"Your dad was bossy because he loved you and feared for your safety. You were running with a dangerous crowd. Although he came across about as subtle as a tank most of the time."

"Amen."

"And he couldn't seem to comprehend that you weren't a new recruit who needed to be broken down and built back up into a team player. The harder he pushed the more you pushed back." She shook her head. "You two were so much alike."

Lauryn gaped. "Daddy and I?"

"Oh yes. Both strong-willed. Both determined to test your limits. The difference is your father found a job that allowed him to channel his wild side and to push himself against the barriers of light, speed and sound—literally."

"I thought my rebelliousness must have come from Adrianna."

"Your father was always a bit untamed."

"But you loved him."

Susan smiled wistfully. "Not at first. Back then we banged heads more often than not. I only married him because I was pregnant and alone and felt I had no other options. But I saw his tender side when he stood by me after I lost my little Daniel and then soon after he brought you home I fell hard. He was a little slower to catch on. But once he did we were good together. I'm gonna miss him for a long time."

Swallowing the sudden lump in her throat, Lauryn covered her mother's hand. Her parents' marriage hadn't begun with love, but it had ended there. Could she hope for the same? Or would Adam never forgive her?

The cab pulled to a stop outside Estate. Lauryn paid the driver, climbed from the car and picked up their luggage. "We'll put these in my office and then find everyone."

The employee entrance was locked at night and she didn't have a key to the exterior doors, so she led Susan past the long line of chicly dressed wannabe guests on the wide sidewalk leading to the front door and stopped in front of the massive guard. "Hi, Deke."

"Lauryn, hey. Been on a trip?"

"Yes, and I brought my mother back with me. Where's Mrs. Garrison's birthday party being held?" She tensed and hoped he didn't refuse to let her in, but he unhooked the rope.

"Upstairs. Red room."

"Thanks."

Inside the music from the downstairs DJ pulsed around them. Lauryn turned away from the milling crowd and used her ID to access a locked door to the offices where she deposited their bags behind her desk. She huffed out a breath and squared her shoulders. Nervousness made her almost queasy.

There was no reason to stall before joining the party. She and her mother had changed into suitable attire at the airport. But she was afraid. Afraid she'd lose Adam tonight. If she hadn't lost him already. But if she didn't go upstairs and try to make this right then she'd definitely need to kiss her heart and her husband goodbye.

"Lauryn?"

"I'm ready, Mom." She retrieved the small gift she'd bought for Bonita from her suitcase. "Let's go crash a party."

His heart wasn't in this.

Adam stood on the sidelines of his mother's birthday bash watching two hundred of Miami's most powerful movers and shakers mingle or dance to the music pulsing through the speakers in the private upstairs room.

He wasn't out there working the crowd, slapping backs, shaking hands and trying to win their confidence for the business council nomination. In fact, he didn't even care whether or not his guests enjoyed themselves. A first for him.

Everyone he'd spoken to had asked for Lauryn. Apparently, her touchy-feely newspaper interview had impressed them.

"Adam," one of his hostess's voice broke into his thoughts, "there's somebody here who insists on speaking to you tonight."

Lauryn? "Who? Where?"

"By the door."

Instead of his wife, Adam spotted Ace Martin, the P.I. Disappointment weighted his shoulders. Disappointment he had no business feeling. He'd told Lauryn not to come. For all he knew she could be in California with Saunders spending forty grand right now.

Was he married or wasn't he? Adam's muscles tensed, but he forced them into action and crossed the room. Had Ace found the answers? Adam wasn't sure what he wanted those answers to be or even if they mattered. His marriage was very likely over either way.

Adam extended his hand. "Ace, thanks for coming."

The P.I. nodded. "Is there someplace private we can talk?"

"My office." He took the freight elevator rather than the stairs. He wasn't in the right frame of mind to charm the guests he'd encounter in the front of the club, and he didn't want to get hung up in a conversation with anyone and delay Ace's revelations even one minute.

The office suite was dark and deserted, but for a second Adam thought he caught a whiff of Lauryn's perfume. *Mind's playing tricks on you, man.* He shook his head. But dammit, he'd missed her. How stupid was that when she'd deceived him and possibly even loved another man?

But when he lay in bed alone at night he kept seeing the honesty in her eyes, and it made him second-guess himself—not a frequent occurrence.

He closed his office door behind Ace.

"Saunders lied," Ace said without preamble. He pulled a file from his briefcase, opened it and spread copies of documents across Adam's desk surface. "Your wife's annulment went through without a hitch. Saunders drugged her just like she said. Medical records backed it up."

Adrenaline shot through Adam. He and Lauryn were still married. Had her claim that she loved him been a lie?

"Every story you asked me to look into checked out. From all accounts, her father was a tough SOB. Rode her hard throughout her teens. She defied him in the typical teenage ways, but other than some underage drinking, never broke the law—or at least there's no record of it. Good student. Popular. Typical kid, if a little on the rowdy side during her high school years.

"Adam, I can't see her being your Garrison, Inc. snitch. Doesn't fit her character. And there's no unexplained money trail."

"What about Saunders?"

"California cops nabbed him yesterday. Dumbnut still had the cash and the forged document on him. He's not the sharpest knife in the drawer. He's offering to return the money in exchange for a lesser charge. Our pretty boy's not too eager to spend more time behind bars. He's been there before for jacking a few cars and dealing drugs."

"Was he alone?"

"Yes. No sign of Lauryn."

Relief coursed through Adam.

Ace closed his briefcase. "Anything else I can do for you?"

Find my wife.

But Adam didn't ask. Even if Ace found Lauryn the P.I. couldn't make her forgive Adam or make her stop caring for her ex.

"Nothing else. Thanks for your help."

"Just doing my job. Nice to find out someone's innocent for a change."

Innocent. But Adam had convicted her. He'd been judge, jury and hangman. She probably hated his guts.

He wrote Martin a check and showed him out. The last thing Adam wanted to do was rejoin the party. He wanted to find Lauryn and apologize.

For doubting her.

For not telling her he loved her.

Too little, too late? Probably. But he had to try.

He returned to the red room and walked right in on Jordon and Emilio Jefferies standing nose-to-nose, fists clenched and looking ready to brawl.

Adam could make out the tone of their angry voices as he approached, but not the words. He had bouncers for this kind of crap, but considering Emilio would soon be family Adam decided to handle it rather than call security and have Jordon turfed.

"Jordon, I don't remember seeing your name on the guest list." And if the man had a spy planted in Garrison, Inc. then he sure as hell wasn't welcome here.

"What? You don't want me to wish your mother a happy sixtieth?"

"If I believed the sentiment was legitimate I might consider it. But I don't. What do you want?"

Jordon's blue eyes scanned the room, alighting on a target Adam couldn't identify in the shifting crowd. "Nothing. Absolutely nothing."

Looking disgusted, he turned on his heel and stormed out.

"Know what that was about?" Adam asked Emilio.

His future brother-in-law hesitated. "No."

Adam would bet his Beemer Emilio Jefferies knew exactly why his brother was here. But pushing for an answer fell right off Adam's priority list when he looked across the room and saw the beautiful blonde standing with his mother and Brooke.

Lauryn had come home.

"You look like her," Bonita Garrison said before Lauryn could escape after delivering the birthday gift and good wishes.

"Who?" Lauryn asked absently. She noted the worried expression on Brooke Garrison's face as Adam's sister stared across the room and looked to see what had caught her attention. Emilio Jefferies and Adam. *Adam.* Lauryn's heart thumped harder, faster and her palms moistened.

"Your mother," Bonita answered, yanking Lauryn's attention back to her. Bonita's eyes, so like Adam's, shifted to Susan Lowes, assessed her and then returned to Lauryn. "Your birthmother. Adrianna Laurence."

Lauryn's throat closed up. She yearned for details, but she didn't want to make Susan uncomfortable by asking for them.

Susan took the initiative. "How so, Mrs. Garrison? I've never seen a picture of Adrianna although my husband did speak of her occasionally."

Bonita looked like she regretted opening the dialogue. Her lips thinned and her gaze drifted to the bar then returned. "The coloring is different. She was as dark as Lauryn is fair. But the bone structure is identical. The profile, the set of your eyes, your chin."

No slurring marred Bonita's clipped words tonight. Lauryn wondered if that was her choice or because Adam controlled the bartenders.

"You knew her?" Lauryn asked with a flutter of excitement in her belly.

"She often accompanied her mother to society functions."

"Really? What was she like?"

"She was quite a trial to her parents, always finding little ways to stir up trouble and draw attention to herself. Reading the interview you did with the paper quite reminded me of her. I trust you've outgrown the need to be the center of attention? Or have you? I'm not sure after this debacle."

"Mother!" Brooke exclaimed.

"I have, Mrs. Garrison. All I want to do now is be a good wife to Adam." *If he'll let me.*

Bonita lifted her chin and looked down her nose at Lauryn.

"Adrianna went out on a limb to save her child. You went out on a limb to save mine. Perhaps you have some redeeming qualities. But that remains to be seen."

"Mother!" Brooke repeated.

"It's okay, Brooke. She's right. I—"

"Lauryn." Adam's voice stalled her racing heart.

She turned and there he was, tall and lean, with his disheveled hair and intensely blue eyes. She flushed hot and then cold. Would he throw her out?

"Tommy lied," she blurted.

"I know." There was something in his eyes, some emotion Lauryn couldn't identify, that made her mouth go dry.

"Adam, get me a gin and tonic. Your bartender refuses to pour."

"Sorry, mother. Everyone has orders to keep you sober tonight." He spoke without looking away from Lauryn.

"Not exactly a happy birthday then, is it?" Bonita sniped and then stalked off. Brooke followed.

Adam shifted his attention to her mother. He extended his hand. "My apologies for my mother's behavior. I'm Adam Garrison."

"Susan Lowes, Lauryn's mother."

Adam's tight smile didn't completely erase the tension in his face. "It's nice to meet you, Mrs. Lowes. You've raised an amazing daughter."

"Yes, I have, haven't I?" Susan squeezed and then released Lauryn's hand. "Lauryn, could you direct me to the powder room?"

Lauryn looked from her mother to Adam and back again. "I'm sorry, I don't know where it is. I don't come upstairs very often."

"That way," Adam pointed toward a set of double doors.

"Thank you." With that Susan turned and left them.

Lauryn wanted to call her back. She wasn't ready for this conversation. Wasn't ready to blow her last chance.

Instead, she squared her shoulders and swallowed to dampen her mouth. "How did you know about Tommy?"

Adam gripped her bicep and led her toward an empty corner where the music and chattering crowd were less intrusive. Once there he didn't release her. She wanted to lean into the warmth of his hand, to grab that hand and never let it go.

"I hired a private investigator."

She couldn't help the flood of disappointment. "I guess it was too much to hope you'd actually believe me."

"Lauryn—"

"It's okay, Adam. I understand. My whole plan to move here, befriend you and search for the diaries was ill-conceived and completely self-centered. I never should have done it. I hurt too many people and I lied too many times."

"You didn't lie, Lauryn. You left things out. Things you didn't consider relevant. And they wouldn't have been if Saunders hadn't decided to twist the facts. Your past, like mine, is part of who you are. We made mistakes, but we learned from them. I changed, and so did you."

He didn't hate her? Her heart swelled with hope. "I didn't expect my past to come back to bite me. But I should have given you the information and let you make the decision. You had the most to lose. The nomination—"

"Forget the nomination. If the council members are too narrow-minded to realize I'm qualified for the job then it's their loss."

"But what about the bigger stake in Garrison, Inc. that you wanted?"

"I'm no longer interested. You were right. I'm doing what I want to do, investing when and how I want to invest, with no one to answer to but myself. And I'm good at it. I've always been a solo player. I shouldn't try to sign up for a team sport now."

"Are you sure?"

"I'm sure." He scanned the crowd and then faced her again. "And I'm not completely blameless in this deal. My reasons for marrying you were…what was it you said? Ill-conceived and completely self-centered."

Did that mean they had a chance or that he was ready to walk away from it all—his plan and her?

"But enough about our mistakes. You know you have every right to contest the settlement of the Laurence estate, don't you? You'd inherit millions."

Her mouth dropped open. She snapped it closed when she realized she was gaping. "I—I didn't know that."

"The estate was supposed to go to the last surviving heir. That's you. After a year's search without finding an heir, the properties were sold, but the monies are currently being managed by a trust."

"Ohmigod. I don't even know what to say to that."

"Think about it. Talk to Brandon. Learn your options."

"Right. Yes. I will." She shook her head. "Why are you telling me this?"

His hand tightened on her arm and then his fingers loosened and massaged tiny circles on the tender underside. Her pulse quickened and tension wound deep inside. "Because you'll be wealthy enough to do whatever you want. To live wherever you want. With whomever you want."

"You know money's not why I wanted to find Adrianna's diaries, don't you? I needed to know I was wanted—that I wasn't a baby even a mother couldn't love."

There. She said it out loud for the first time and found understanding in Adam's eyes.

After several silent seconds he nodded. His hand slid down

the length of her arm until he captured her fingers. He stroked her knuckle above her wedding rings with his thumb.

"The P.I. told me the police arrested Saunders in California yesterday. Saunders has already turned over the money. He'll be shipped back here to face extortion charges." Adam's throat worked as he swallowed. "Unless you want the charges dropped."

Confused, Lauryn frowned. "Why would I want them dropped?"

"Because you still care about him. I know you filed charges to help me, but if you want a future with him, then I don't want you to be an inmate's wife, and I don't want you to waste your inheritance on his legal fees."

Alarm prickled through her. Did Adam still want the divorce? "Adam, I don't care about Tommy, and I don't want to drop the charges. What he did was illegal and he hurt you."

"Then why did you hesitate when I asked you to write down information about him for the police?"

She flashed back to their last morning together in the Sunset Island house—the last morning she'd been happy.

"Because I realized at that moment that everything my father had bellowed at me was right. I was headed down a dangerous path. If I'd stayed with Tommy I'd very likely have been in jail by now. I may not have been born a baby a mother couldn't love, but for five years I did my best to become a teenager a father couldn't. I'm very lucky he and my mother cared enough to stand by me when I was trying so hard to push them away."

Adam's hand tightened around hers. "You didn't hesitate because you loved Saunders?"

The intensity of his gaze tripped her pulse. "How could I when…I love you? But I know I messed up by keeping secrets. And I know you might not be able to forgive me or trust me again. So, Adam…if it's what you want…I'll give you your freedom. But I really want to try to make this marriage work."

He closed his eyes and inhaled deeply. When he lifted his lids again Lauryn's knees nearly buckled at the love she saw shining back at her. Beaming at her. Like a lighthouse beacon.

She mashed her lips together and pressed a fist over her heart. Hope swelled within her like a hot air balloon, making her feel light-headed.

Adam cupped Lauryn's shoulders. "If you can forgive me for being a total ass even when your eyes and my heart told me to trust you, then I want to renegotiate our agreement."

She shifted uneasily. "Renegotiate how exactly?"

"Two years is not enough. Hell, fifty years isn't going to be enough. I want eternity. Not one second less." He lifted her hand to his mouth and kissed her knuckles. "I want these rings to mean the words we said on that beach."

He released her hand only to gently cradle her face and brush his thumbs over her damp cheeks. She hadn't even noticed the tears escaping.

"I love you, Lauryn Garrison. I want to spend the rest of my life showing you that you are wanted. Loved. Needed. And if you're willing, I want to fill your birthmother's house with her grandchildren."

Her lips quivered and happiness blossomed inside her. She took a ragged breath. "On one condition."

"Name it."

"You don't pay me to be your wife. That's one job I'd willingly do for free."

He winked and her heart turned over. "You have yourself a deal, sweetheart, and I'm going to make sure it's one deal you will never regret."

* * * * *

SPECIAL EDITION®

LIFE, LOVE AND FAMILY

*These contemporary romances will strike a chord
with you as heroines juggle life
and relationships on their way to true love.*

New York Times *bestselling author Linda Lael Miller
brings you a BRAND-NEW contemporary story
featuring her fan-favorite McKettrick family.*

Meg McKettrick is surprised to be reunited with her
high school flame, Brad O'Ballivan. After enjoying a
career as a country-and-western singer, Brad aches for
a home and family…and seeing Meg again makes him
realize he still loves her. But their pride manages to inter-
fere with love…until an unexpected matchmaker gets
involved.

*Turn the page for a sneak preview of
THE McKETTRICK WAY
by Linda Lael Miller
On sale November 20,
wherever books are sold.*

Brad shoved the truck into gear and drove to the bottom of the hill, where the road forked. Turn left, and he'd be home in five minutes. Turn right, and he was headed for Indian Rock.

He had no damn business going to Indian Rock.

He had nothing to say to Meg McKettrick, and if he never set eyes on the woman again, it would be two weeks too soon.

He turned right.

He couldn't have said why.

He just drove straight to the Dixie Dog Drive-In.

Back in the day, he and Meg used to meet at the Dixie Dog, by tacit agreement, when either of them had been away. It had been some kind of universe thing, purely intuitive.

Passing familiar landmarks, Brad told himself he ought to turn around. The old days were gone. Things had ended badly between him and Meg anyhow, and she wasn't going to be at the Dixie Dog.

He kept driving.

He rounded a bend, and there was the Dixie Dog. Its big neon sign, a giant hot dog, was all lit up and going through its corny sequence—first it was covered in red squiggles of light, meant to suggest ketchup, and then yellow, for mustard.

Brad pulled into one of the slots next to a speaker, rolled down the truck window and ordered.

A girl roller-skated out with the order about five minutes later.

When she wheeled up to the driver's window, smiling, her eyes went wide with recognition, and she dropped the tray with a clatter.

Silently Brad swore. Damn if he hadn't forgotten he was a famous country singer.

The girl, a skinny thing wearing too much eye makeup, immediately started to cry. "I'm sorry!" she sobbed, squatting to gather up the mess.

"It's okay," Brad answered quietly, leaning to look down at her, catching a glimpse of her plastic name tag. "It's okay, Mandy. No harm done."

"I'll get you another dog and a shake right away, Mr. O'Ballivan!"

"Mandy?"

She stared up at him pitifully, sniffling. Thanks to the copious tears, most of the goop on her eyes had slid south. "Yes?"

"When you go back inside, could you not mention seeing me?"

"But you're Brad O'Ballivan!"

"Yeah," he answered, suppressing a sigh. "I know."

She rolled a little closer. "You wouldn't happen to have a picture you could autograph for me, would you?"

"Not with me," Brad answered.

"You could sign this napkin, though," Mandy said. "It's only got a little chocolate on the corner."

Brad took the paper napkin and her order pen, and scrawled his name. Handed both items back through the window.

She turned and whizzed back toward the side entrance to the Dixie Dog.

Brad waited, marveling that he hadn't considered incidents like this one before he'd decided to come back home. In retrospect, it seemed shortsighted, to say the least, but the truth was, he'd expected to be—Brad O'Ballivan.

Presently Mandy skated back out again, and this time she managed to hold on to the tray.

"I didn't tell a soul!" she whispered. "But Heather and Darlene *both* asked me why my mascara was all smeared." Efficiently she hooked the tray onto the bottom edge of the window.

Brad extended payment, but Mandy shook her head.

"The boss said it's on the house, since I dumped your first order on the ground."

He smiled. "Okay, then. Thanks."

Mandy retreated, and Brad was just reaching for the food when a bright red Blazer whipped into the space beside his. The driver's door sprang open, crashing into the metal speaker, and somebody got out in a hurry.

Something quickened inside Brad.

And in the next moment Meg McKettrick was standing practically on his running board, her blue eyes blazing.

Brad grinned. "I guess you're not over me after all," he said.

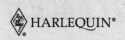

American ★ Romance®

Kate Merrill had grown up convinced
that the most attractive men were incapable
of ever settling down. Yet the harder she
resisted the superstar photographer
Tyler Nichols, the more persistent the
handsome world traveler became.
So by the time Christmas arrived, there
was only one wish on her holiday list—
that she was wrong!

LOOK FOR

THE CHRISTMAS DATE

BY

Michele Dunaway

**Available December
wherever you buy books**

www.eHarlequin.com   HAR75195

REQUEST YOUR FREE BOOKS!

2 FREE NOVELS PLUS 2 FREE GIFTS!

Silhouette Desire®

Passionate, Powerful, Provocative!

YES! Please send me 2 FREE Silhouette Desire® novels and my 2 FREE gifts. After receiving them, if I don't wish to receive any more books, I can return the shipping statement marked "cancel." If I don't cancel, I will receive 6 brand-new novels every month and be billed just $3.80 per book in the U.S., or $4.47 per book in Canada, plus 25¢ shipping and handling per book and applicable taxes, if any*. That's a savings of almost 15% off the cover price! I understand that accepting the 2 free books and gifts places me under no obligation to buy anything. I can always return a shipment and cancel at any time. Even if I never buy another book from Silhouette, the two free books and gifts are mine to keep forever.

225 SDN EEXJ 326 SDN EEXU

Name	(PLEASE PRINT)	
Address		Apt.
City	State/Prov.	Zip/Postal Code

Signature (if under 18, a parent or guardian must sign)

Mail to the **Silhouette Reader Service™**:
IN U.S.A.: P.O. Box 1867, Buffalo, NY 14240-1867
IN CANADA: P.O. Box 609, Fort Erie, Ontario L2A 5X3

Not valid to current Silhouette Desire subscribers.

Want to try two free books from another line?
Call 1-800-873-8635 or visit www.morefreebooks.com.

* Terms and prices subject to change without notice. NY residents add applicable sales tax. Canadian residents will be charged applicable provincial taxes and GST. This offer is limited to one order per household. All orders subject to approval. Credit or debit balances in a customer's account(s) may be offset by any other outstanding balance owed by or to the customer. Please allow 4 to 6 weeks for delivery.

Your Privacy: Silhouette is committed to protecting your privacy. Our Privacy Policy is available online at www.eHarlequin.com or upon request from the Reader Service. From time to time we make our lists of customers available to reputable firms who may have a product or service of interest to you. If you would prefer we not share your name and address, please check here. ☐

SDES07

Inside ROMANCE

Stay up-to-date on all your romance reading news!

Inside Romance is a FREE quarterly newsletter highlighting our upcoming series releases and promotions.

Visit
www.eHarlequin.com/InsideRomance
to sign up to receive our complimentary newsletter today!

IRN1107

Get ready to meet

THREE WISE WOMEN

with stories by

DONNA BIRDSELL, LISA CHILDS

and

SUSAN CROSBY.

Don't miss these three unforgettable stories
about modern-day women and the love
and new lives they find on Christmas.

Look for *Three Wise Women*
Available December wherever you buy books.

Introducing

a brand-new miniseries with light-hearted
and playful stories that will make you Blush...
because who says that sex has to be serious?

Starting in December with...

BABY, IT'S COLD OUTSIDE
by Cathy Yardley

Chilly temperatures send Colin Reeves and
Emily Stanfield indoors—then it's sparks, sensual
heat and hot times ahead! But will their private
holiday hometown reunion last longer than
forty-eight delicious hours in bed?

COMING NEXT MONTH